AF419890

Esther's Story

Book two in The Woodcarver's Quilt series,
by J. Linde

Author Dedication

Esther's Story is dedicated to all Foster
and
Adoptive families who have and continue
to make a difference in a child's life. I
also
want to thank Social Service offices who
work tirelessly, making sure children
have a
voice

God bless you.

Table of Contents

Chapter 1 It Begins at Home 9

Chapter 2 The Home Coming 19

Chapter 3 Home Again 28

Chapter 4 Home is Where the Heart Is 36

Chapter 5 It All Begins at Home 49

Chapter 6 Lessons at Home 62

Chapter 7 Love at Home 75

Chapter 8 Safely Home 91

Chapter 9 Instruction at Home 107

Chapter 10 Education at Home 113

Chapter 11 A Home for Eli 120

Chapter 12 Perusing the New Home 135

Chapter 13 Home for Supper 149

Chapter 14 Home Cookin' 158

Chapter 15 Time to Come Home 167

Chapter 16 Home for Christmas 177

Chapter 17 New Ideas for Home 186

Chapter 18 Twyla Laine 196

Chapter 19 Home to Stay 204

Epilogue 215

CHAPTER 1
It Begins at Home

Jed sat on the wooden seat in the old shanty, housing the phone – their one connection to the outside world. Most of the messages on the recording machine were solicitors. "How on earth did they ever get this phone number?" He impatiently pushed the delete button on the device, then pushed it again. He was about to press the button once more, but the following voice didn't have that robotic monotone. His finger stopped, suspended over the delete key, and he listened while the last message played.

"This message is for Jedidiah and Eva Kuepfer. It's Betsy Ryan from Social Services in Etobicoke. Would you give me a call at your earliest convenience?" – the message ended with a phone number where she could be reached.

There was no need for Jed to jot the number down, but out of habit, he did anyway. He knew the voice, the person it belonged to, and the phone number well. It belonged to a woman in her late thirties or early forties. Betsy Ryan often had a harried look about her because she worried so much about the children in her care – children lost in the system, waiting and hoping for responsible foster homes, but preferably loving adoptive families.

Jed listened to the message three times, afraid of missing a single detail. It was a basic, generic message, a message anyone might have heard, but unless the party for whom it was intended received it, it would make no earthly sense. To Jed, the fact that Betsy Ryan had called relayed the urgency for which it was designed. However, there was one problem - the message had been left on the answering machine five days ago, on Monday! He scolded himself mentally. 'I should have been checking the shanty phone regularly.' Only, he hadn't; there had been no reason to. 'There's no sense crying over spilled *milch* – what's done, is done, but how to remedy it?'

Life on an Amish farm in southern Ontario could be hectic at times, and they had just finished bringing in their first cutting of hay for the year. Jed made a beeline for the house. This matter was something he needed to share with Eva. They made few decisions without consulting with one another. On the way, he called out to Eli. "I'll be back in a few minutes, *sohn*. Go ahead and fill up the water troughs."

"*Ja, Dat*. I'll look after it," the boy, tall for his age, turned back to his chores of feeding the calves and pumping water into the long, galvanized tanks.

Jed kicked his boots off at the back door and padded into the kitchen in stocking feet. Momentarily, his mission was forgotten as he took a deep breath, inhaling the warm smell of baking bread. As long as he lived, he knew he would never get tired of the smell of freshly baked bread. His mother looked up from rolling pie dough with the wooden rolling pin. Eva, his wife of seven years, glanced at the tall pendulum clock standing stately in the corner of their spacious kitchen. 'Jed's early for his mid-morning break,' she reasoned silently, smiling at him and dusting the flour from her hands. "Thirsty, already?"

"*Ja*, but that's not why I came in," Jed was drawn back to the present by Eva's question.

"Eli, okay?"

"*Ja*. He's feedin' the calves."

She looked at him quizzically, wondering what they owed the pleasure of his early mid-morning appearance.

"We got a phone call from Betsy Ryan."

Instantly, the color drained from Eva's face. His mother stopped rolling out the dough, and both women's mouths fell ajar.

"Did she say what she wanted?" Eva finally found her voice to ask.

"Just ta call her at our earliest convenience, but that was five days ago."

"You don't suppose they want to take Eli from us, do you?" Eva had a petrified look on her face.

"She didn't say, but they can't take him! We adopted him. He belongs here with us!"

"We should call her right away," Eva ignored his attempt to reassure her.

"*Ja*. We need ta return her call, tagether. It's been five days, but we can call anyway. Fridays are always busy fer them, doin' paperwork, an' such, before the weekend."

Eva nodded and glanced over at May.

"Go and see what she wants, or we'll be wondering and stewing all weekend. I'll keep an eye on the bread," the older woman instructed.

Jed and Eva nodded, left the kitchen, and walked purposefully toward the phone shanty.

Seven-year-old Eli watched his parents step off the back porch and hurry toward the phone shed. His eyebrows gathered in a frown. 'Must be somethin' real important, 'cause *Mamm* didn't even remove her chorin' apron.' He turned his attention back to finish watering off the calves. 'It don't make any sense ta me,' he mulled over his parents' uncharacteristic behavior. 'There's only room fer one in the shed. One of them will have ta stand outside, an' that one will be *Mamm* because *Dat* is the one who always makes the calls. I don't ever remember *Mamm* usin' the phone.' The more Eli thought about it, the more curious he became, and he ran hard to catch up with them.

Jed consulted the phone number he'd jotted on the paper pad and set the rotary dial into motion. He waited patiently while it repeatedly rang on the other end.

Eventually, a woman's lethargic voice answered, and he was asked to wait.

"Somebody's there," he murmured in a low voice while covering the mouthpiece with his hand. "The operator asked me ta hold the line while they put us through."

Eva nodded her head in understanding.

"*Ja*, this is Jed Kuepfer, returnin' Betsy Ryan's call," he turned and responded to the unseen person on the other end of the line. Again, he covered the mouthpiece. "She's in the office; they're puttin' us through now," he relayed for Eva's benefit.

"*Ja*, this is Jed an' Eva Kuepfer returnin' yer call." There was a short pause on Jed's part, then, "*Ja*, we are *gut. Ja*, Eli is *gut*. He got himself some calves."

Eva stood listening to the one-sided conversation; her eyebrows were drawn together in a frown as she held her breath.

"*Ach*, that's not *gut*. I'm sorry ta hear that," Jed's voice was sympathetic.

Eva placed her hands tightly against her chest and leaned heavily against the door frame of the hut, expecting the worst.

"*Ja*, just a minute, an' I'll see if'n we can get away."

By this time, Eva was expecting the worst possible news.

"Betsy wants us ta go in – sooner, the better. They got a *boppli* they want us ta take. She said the *boppli* has something called failure ta thrive. They'll send a car if'n we can go taday."

By this point, Eva was close to collapsing. "They don't want to take Eli from us? They want to give us another *boppli*? *Danke* heavenly *Vater*," she whispered close to tears. "*Ja*. Of course, we'll go," she nodded, tears rolling down her cheeks. She heard Jed say, as if far, far away. "*Ja,* we will be ready 'round noon."

Jed returned the receiver to the phone cradle and stepped out of the shed.

"I thought they were going to take Eli," Eva leaned against him, resting her forehead against his shoulder.

"*Nee*, they want us ta raise another," Jed patted her back, comforting her.

At that moment, Eli stood before them, tears streaming down his face. "I don't want ta go back so ya can raise another."

"*Nee, sohn.* We're not takin' ya back. Yer stayin' here with us," Jed tried to reason with the upset child.

"That's not what ya said. Yer goin' ta get a *boppli*. I heard ya," he wailed. "I heard ya. Ya don't want me anymore. I tried ta be *gut Dat*. Honest, I was tryin' real hard," Eli cried, large forlorn tears continuing down his face.

Jed held the child close. "*Sohn*, we're not sendin' ya back. Remember how happy ya were when ya had a ferever home with us."

"Ja," Eli nodded, his tear-streaked face buried in Jed's shirt.

"Well, we have this big *alt* farm. Don't ya think it's big enough fer one more *boppli*, ta give it a ferever home too?"

"I guess." Eli consented begrudgingly at the thought while continuing to hold onto Jed.

Eva rubbed him consolingly on the back, "we're going in to talk to the lady about the *boppli,* and you can *kumme* too if you want." She smiled encouragingly down at her son.

"*Nee.*" Eli looked up at them with haunted eyes. "I need ta stay here."

Jed nodded, "*Ja, das gut.* Ya can stay an' help *Dawdi* with the chores. We might be late gettin' back anyway."

"Ya promise ta *kumme* back?" Eli wrapped his arms around his parents with a strength that stemmed from fear.

"*Ja,* I promise we'll be back. Maybe with a *bruder* or *schwester.* Will you help us with the *boppli*? Can we count on your help?" Eva rubbed his back lovingly.

"As long as I don't have ta change its *windel,*" Eli's nose turned up at the thought of changing the baby's diaper.

"*Nee,* ya won't have ta change its *windel,*" Jed laughed over the top of Eli's head toward Eva.

"An' I don't want it sleepin' in my room, either," he demanded further.

"*Nee.* The *boppli* will have its own room," Eva continued to console.

Eli gave a great sigh of relief. "*Danke.*"

"*Kumme*," Jed wrapped one arm around Eli and the other about Eva leading them toward their century-old two-story farmhouse. "My stomach says it must be close ta lunchtime, 'specially if'n the driver is *kummin'* after lunch." They walked back toward the house together.

~.~.~.~

After lunch, Eva and Jed sat on the porch waiting for their ride to come. The time seemed to drag by. Lost in thought, they watched as the wind blew the branches back and forth on the old maple tree.

May had made sticky buns; she wrapped a couple in paper and placed the bag in Eli's hand. "Special for you, 'cause you're special to me."

"*Danke Mammi*," he hugged her around the neck and ran out the kitchen door. The breeze caught the brim of his straw hat and tumbled it across the yard, revealing unruly jet-black curly hair. Eva and Jed smiled and chuckled while watching him chase after the straw hat, but the wind tumbled it a little further across the yard every time he got close to it. Finally, the fencing around the yard caught it and held onto it so he could snatch it up. "*Dawdi*, wait fer me!" He called after his granddad's retreating back.

"Just as well he'll be stayin' home. It might be late before we get back," Jed smiled as they watched Eli disappear into the barn.

"*Ja*. He'd be fretting the whole time. At least he has

some security here with your *Mamm* and *Daed*," Eva
agreed.

"*Ja*," Jed said aloud, then nodded toward the road.
"That looks like our ride now." A van slowed to turn into
the farm and crept up the lane.

Jed and Eva stood up from the swing seat, called into
the house that they would be leaving, and stepped off the
porch to meet the driver.

A man in his late forties got out of the van. "This the
Kuepfer place?" He looked at the piece of paper in his
hand, then up at Jed and Eva, as if somehow the
information would match the couple standing before him.

"*Ja*, we are Jed an' Eva Kuepfer," Jed returned with a
quick nod.

"Good," the man gave a relieved smile. "I'm Mac, your
driver," he opened the van's side door revealing wide,
leather-covered seats. Jed helped Eva climb in before
joining her on the bench seat. Mac slammed the heavy
door behind them with a sense of finality as they settled in
for the drive.

Their driver got behind the steering wheel. "I never
know if these instructions will get me where I need to go,
but these were accurate, almost to a fault," he chuckled.
"There's no room for guesswork when I'm driving this
far," he held up the sheet of paper with its directions. They
watched as he leaned sideways, opened a small door in the
van's dash, and threw the driving instructions into the
yawning compartment before shutting the metal door.

"Might need that to bring you back," he explained. "It'll take us a little over two hours. It's about a hundred and twenty miles. I hope you don't mind if I listen to some music? It helps to take the monotony out of driving."

"*Ja, das gut,*" Jed nodded, although he and Eva exchanged a look. They hoped their driver's music wouldn't be too loud or obnoxious. As it turned out, Mac was respectful of his passengers and kept the volume of the music turned down. They watched as he drummed his fingers on the steering wheel, keeping in rhythm with the music as he drove.

~ ~ ~

Fear not, for I am with thee:
Be not dismayed; for I am thy God:
I will strengthen thee; yea, I will help thee
~ Isaiah 41:10 ~

CHAPTER 2
The Home Coming

It seemed forever before Mac finally pulled into the parking lot of Social Services in Etobicoke. It had been two years since another driver had driven Jed and Eva to this same parking lot to meet Eli and take him home. Garbage was strewn everywhere, and weeds were growing between the cracks in the pavement. They looked out the van's windows, noting nothing had changed.

"Just go through that green door," Mac nodded toward a door with mesh embedded in the glass. "I'll be back to take you home when you're ready to go." At Jed's questioning look, he supplied, "they'll give me a call when you're ready to leave."

"*Danke*," Jed nodded understanding and ensured Eva safely got out of the van.

As they passed through the heavy green metal door, they soon realized that, like the parking lot, the room inside the door had remained the same. It was hot and close; the only relief came from a fan droning in the corner of the room. It kept the large reception area from becoming too unbearably hot. If one thought about it, all the fan succeeded in circulating was hot air from one side of the room to the other and then back again.

They walked over to the receptionist sitting behind a low, sterile-looking white partition. Jed announced, "We're Jed an' Eva Kuepfer, *kumme* ta see Betsy Ryan."

"Yes, just take a seat, Mr. Kuepfer, and I'll let Betsy know you're here," the woman stood up and went through a swinging door to an area that housed different offices. Within minutes, the two-way swinging door was pushed open again, and sailing through it came Betsy Ryan.

"It's so good to see you both again," she extended her hand first to Eva and then to Jed. "And I'm so glad you could come as quickly as you did. Come with me, and I'll fill you in on the baby."

Eva let out a long sigh of relief, knowing that her hopes were about to be realized, and smiled at Jed. He nodded, his facial features softening. They followed the caseworker back to an office area with a desk piled high with files. Jed and Eva stared at the pile in awe, wondering how it stayed upright; it had such a precarious lean. Those files represented children waiting to have their cases heard. The fate of so many had been and would be decided upon on that very desk.

Betsy invited them to sit while she sat in her chair behind the desk and opened a folder. "As you know, it is Social Services' policy never to reveal the background of the children placed in homes by our services." Jed and Eva nodded their understanding; it had been the same with Eli.

"As you also know, our policy is to place a child in a home on a probationary period." Betsy looked from one to the other with intensity. "However, there are always exceptions. This time is one of those rare exceptions! I fervently hope that I won't receive a phone call from you within that probationary period that you are not interested in keeping the child."

Eva looked at Jed, alarmed at the tone in Betsy's voice and that someone would send a child back as easily as some would dicker and barter over livestock.

"I can tell you this," Betsy continued, "The baby was born to an unmarried woman, not much more than a child herself. The mother has elected to put her career before the child so that she can have a family when she is older and has gained financial security." She didn't pause to examine the pained expressions of the couple sitting across the desk from her; she had seen it countless times. "In the past, the child has been in different foster homes while we worked with the mother, hoping to encourage a permanent reunion with the two."

Betsy glanced at a report in the folder, "all foster parents relate the child is irritable, refuses to eat, and is malnourished, as a result." She flipped through additional reports in the file and added, "is a restless sleeper and cries a lot." She looked up from the thick sheaf of papers, adding, "the baby has been examined by one of our physicians, and blood work was conducted to rule out contracted diseases. Nothing was revealed from the family history provided by the birth mother regarding hereditary diseases. If we cannot find a permanent, loving home, this child's future is not promising, and the prognosis is grave. As I told you over the phone," she looked at Jed, "the diagnosis given by the examining physician is Failure to Thrive. That's all I can tell you." Closing the folder, she inquired, "would you like some time to talk about the baby and what adjustments you and your family will have to make?"

Eva turned hopeful eyes toward Jed, an element of sadness registering there. His eyes were filled with empathy as he returned Eva's gaze. He raised his one eyebrow fractionally, and she touched his shirt sleeve. Years of knowing one another afforded them a silent communication only the two understood. Their wordless expressions spoke volumes as if words had actually been said. Jed turned to look at the social worker sitting across the desk. Betsy's eyes registered cautious hope at his following words, "When can we meet the little one?"

Betsy's tired face broke into a relieved smile. "Thank you. Thank you so much," she pushed back from her desk. "I know if anyone can help this child, you and Eva can. That is why I called you, but I don't mind admitting I was getting concerned when you didn't return my call. Come with me to the family room." Standing, she led the way down a long hall to a room lit with artificial lighting where children were playing, some with adults. Jed wondered if the adults were potential foster or adoptive parents. Betsy approached one of the childcare workers, who pointed to a row of cribs. Turning, Betsy smiled toward Jed and Eva, and together they approached a white sterile-looking crib. Laying in a fetal position was a thin, pale baby. The child was awake but seemed to stare at nothing. Not even their movement as they drew near the crib was a distraction to the child, who continued staring into thin air.

Eva placed her hand on Jed's arm. "Our *tochter*," she whispered close to tears.

"Can we pick her up?" Jed asked the social worker as he continued looking down at the baby.

"Yes, but I'll warn you, be prepared for her to cry. She doesn't like being held," Betsy cautioned.

Jed leaned over the high side of the crib and rubbed the baby's back. "*Hallo*, little one," he murmured.

"How old is she?" Eva asked, without taking her eyes off the child.

"Not quite two yet. I'll give you her birthdate and immunization record before you leave. The doctor says she's functioning at about the twelve-month level. Betsy advocated for the child, "All she needs is someone to love her and not give up on her."

Jed reached over the bars with both arms and gently cradled the baby in his hands; it seemed she weighed less than a feather. She let out a weak whimper and turned her head away from him. She smelled sour of old vomit, and her clothes reeked of old musty urine.

"Can I change her before we leave?" Eva asked,

rubbing her fingers over the little girl's thick curls. The neglected state of the baby broke her heart, and she glanced up to blink her tears away. Immediately she noticed the sheer amount of children needing care, as opposed to the few adults available to care for them.

"Yes, there are changing tables against the wall and diapers folded beside the tables."

"Do you have warm water so that I can wash her?" Eva looked hopefully at Betsy.

"Yes, there are water taps on that wall and basins beneath the sink," Betsy pointed out.

Jed held the baby close as she continued to emit weak, pathetic cries while Eva prepared the area to wash and change her. She had packed a little bag with a soft cotton nightgown and a flannel blanket, not knowing what to bring because the child's age had not been revealed to them. The plain nightgown would be too big on the baby. Eva looked with disgust; at least it was better than the garment with the sour-smelling dried-on regurgitated food.

Eva worked quickly, washing and changing the baby, while Jed ensured she didn't roll off the table. The entire time Eva worked to dress her, the little girl cried, miserable as she attempted to move away from their gentle hands.

'Dear heavenly *Vater*, please help us. What should we do?' Jed prayed silently, and just as quickly came the answer, 'pick her up and rock her.' He obeyed, holding her close, rubbing her back, and rocking his body back and forth to soothe her. Eva tucked a clean diaper between the little girl's face and Jed's shirt. "Let me braid her hair while you're holding her. We will wash it when we get home. *Ja*?"

"*Ja*," he agreed and continued to roll from one foot to the other, doing his best to rock the child. Eventually, the baby stopped crying and began to hiccup. She held onto Jed's shirt with a death-like grip, a vise-like hold he knew would be hard to break free from, but he didn't care. If it gave her comfort to cling to him, he wouldn't take that from her. So, the inseparable bond between the two began that only death could hope to separate.

Eva quickly braided the thick curly locks, and within minutes she looked like a little Amish girl, albeit a rather sickly one. Jed placed the baby in Eva's outstretched arms. "If she gets too heavy, I'll hold her for ya," he offered, suddenly missing the little fingers clinging to him. Eva rubbed the baby's back and rocked her to comfort her.

After completing much paperwork with Betsy, she handed them a bag with the agency's logo stamped on the outside. "This is the package we send home with all new parents and an envelope with a copy of her birth certificate and immunization record. Anything else, we will mail it to you. We will keep in touch, and a visiting nurse will stop by one day next week to see how you are making out. If you have any concerns, get in touch with me right away. You know the routine from adopting Eli."

Jed and Eva nodded in understanding and followed the

caseworker back down the hall, through the reception area to the parking lot where the van was waiting for them. They said their goodbyes and climbed back into the passenger van, Jed making sure Eva and the baby were settled safely on the seat. Mac securely closed the van door behind them.

The drive home would be long, but Jed and Eva didn't care. They were bringing home a daughter, a sister for Eli, and a grandchild for Jed's parents. Jed grinned, '*Mamm* will have an *enkelin* ta spoil.'

"What's her name?" Mac asked over his shoulder before pulling out of the Social Services parking lot.

Jed and Eva looked at each other, thinking, 'a name?' They hadn't given it any thought. They were so happy to be bringing home another child they hadn't given the baby's name any idea, and Betsy hadn't supplied them with one.

Jed nodded to Eva, "what do you think?"

She smiled and looked hopeful, "Esther?"

He nodded his head in approval. "*Ja*, Esther is a *gut* name."

"That's a good name," Mac agreed with a smile. "Well, little Miss. Esther. You hold tight, and we'll have you home in a couple of hours." After that, he concentrated on his driving. They were headed west into the sun on a late Friday afternoon. Traffic was crazy, but he drove defensively – after all, he had precious cargo on board.

Eva smiled and quietly murmured, "Esther was adopted

by her onkle Mordecai in the Bible; her name means secret because Mordecai forbade her to reveal her family background. Now, *Gott* has blessed us with a secret. One of His blessed children."

An hour later, Jed lifted a sleeping Esther from Eva's arms. "*Danke*," she murmured. "My arms were beginning to fall asleep." Turning, she brushed Esther's hair away from her face as she slept.

Curious, Eva pulled the copy of Esther's birth certificate from Betsy's envelope. "*Ach*, look at this!" Eva showed the paper to Jed, excited. "Esther was born the day we adopted Eli! *Gott* knew even then that she would be our *tochter*." Tears pooled in her eyes as she leaned over and showed the birth certificate to Jed. "She was *Gott's* secret all this time, and we didn't know a thing about her until today."

"*Ja,* we are blessed," Jed agreed. "He is *gut*, ain't?"

"*Ja*, all the time," Eva smiled and touched the sleeping baby on the cheek. "Her hair is the color of your beard," she looked closely, trying to distinguish between the two.

"I wondered why ya kept tuggin' at it when ya was braidin' her hair." They both chuckled silently at the humor of Jed's beard being braided into Esther's hair.

~ ~ ~

The Lord watches over and sustains the fatherless...
~ Psalm 146:9 ~

CHAPTER 3
Home Again

Mac turned his van up the Kuepfer lane. He had spent long hours driving that day and wasn't finished yet; there was still the return trip to make. Eva glanced at Mac's tired face in the rearview mirror. 'I can't imagine how tired he must be.' Aloud she sympathized, "all of that driving has got to be tiring." She let out a deep sigh of exhaustion. "Even though I am only a passenger, I can't imagine sitting behind a steering wheel for hours on end, barely able to move or reposition myself. And to imagine you have to keep your leg stretched out all the time to keep the car moving forward. To do that for all these hours must be beyond tiring, to say the least!"

Mac nodded in appreciation at her kind words. "I'm happy to help you."

Jed leaned forward and handed Mac some bills before opening the van's door. "No, that isn't necessary," he protested. "Social Services pay me by the mile for making these trips."

"But, did they buy ya somethin' ta eat taday?" Jed persisted, pushing the money closer to Mac.

"Well, no," he hesitantly admitted with a shrug.

"Then stop an' get yerself somethin'," Jed insisted. "Ya've been drivin' all day." He carefully stepped out of the van, not wanting to wake the sleeping baby in his arms.

"Wait here, and I'll get some sticky buns to take with you," Eva offered and quickly climbed out of the van. She returned minutes later and pressed a package that smelled of cinnamon and hominess into his hand. "*Danke,* for all you have done for us today," she expressed her gratitude.

They said their goodbyes and stepped back while the van pulled away. Jed's parents and Eli joined Jed and Eva to watch the van disappear down the drive. As dusk gathered, the luminous red of the brake lights glowed when Mac stopped at the end of the drive before pulling out onto the road. It was the last they saw of the van before everyone crowded closer to look at the newest member of their family. But Esther, not cooperating, kept her face hidden against Jed's shirt.

Even though the sun hadn't yet set, the evening dampness rolled in off the Great Lakes. It crept like fingers across the fields in the form of dew covering the ground. "*Kumme,* we should go inside," May shepherded them toward the house. "Have you eaten yet?"

"*Nee,* not since lunch." Eva returned, glad to have her feet on solid ground.

Gideon peeked around his son's shoulder, unsuccessfully trying to see Esther's face. "What about the *boppli*? Has she eaten?"

"We'll need to find something for her to eat, too." Eva took a moment to rub her little girl's back lovingly before getting down to business.

"Maybe we could offer her a little sweet water," May suggested.

Jed continued walking toward the house, carrying Esther protectively in his arms. Eva and his mother hurried ahead to prepare the warm water and honey.

"Eli, run over to *Tante* Miriam's and ask her for a bottle. Also, you better ask her if she can spare some *boppli* cereal. She should have both for Ruthie," Eva instructed before disappearing into the house.

"*Ja, Mamm*," Eli acknowledged and sprinted down the drive to their neighbors across the road, returning fifteen minutes later with a bottle, nipple, and rice formula.

"I'll cook a little of the cereal," May offered, "while you put the sweet water in the bottle."

Eva carefully poured the honey water into the bottle, sat next to Jed and rubbed Esther's back.

"Let me turn her, so she's facin' ya," Jed suggested. "If'n she sees the bottle, she might take it on her own." He turned Esther toward Eva, and as predicted, Esther reached for the bottle and began guzzling the water.

"Not too fast!" May warned from the stove as she continued stirring the cereal. "You don't want her to bring it all back up. It doesn't look like she's eaten in days."

"She hasn't." Eva acknowledged gravely, pulling the nipple gently from Esther's mouth. "Betsy Ryan said she has something called Failure to Thrive."

"Then they don't know how ta feed a *boppli*," Gideon exclaimed, perturbed. "We'll feed her up in no time."

Eva tried to place a teaspoon covered with a bit of rice cereal in Esther's mouth, but the baby turned her head away. "She hasn't eaten all day. She should be hungry!" Eva agonized, looking at Jed's parents and then at her husband.

"Put some honey in it," Jed's dad suggested. "Then dip yer finger inta it an' put some on her lips. Once she gets the taste, she'll eat it quick enough."

It was a family affair getting Esther to eat. After two mouthfuls of the sweetened cereal, she turned her head away and reached for the bottle again.

"*Ach*. She surely does smell sour. Ain't so?" May exclaimed, grimacing while shaking her head.

"She needs to have her hair washed and given a *gut* soaking," Eva agreed. "But I'm not sure we can separate her from Jed long enough to do it," she added, half joking.

Jed looked over at Eli. "Before ya go off ta bed, do ya need a snack, *sohn*?"

"*Nee, Dat. Mammi* fed *Dawdi* an' me real *gut* while ya was away."

"Then get the Bible, an' I'll read before ya get on up ta bed. Mornin' *kummes* early. *Ja*?"

"Can I watch the *boppli* have a bath?" Eli asked, not wanting to be excluded from helping with the baby.

"It's not a *gut* place fer a *mann* ta be when womenfolk are bathin'." Jed looked at Eli and raised his eyebrows.

"But *Dat*, she's just a *boppli*," Eli protested.

"Next time yer havin' a bath, how'd be if'n the womenfolk sit 'round an' watch ya while ya have no clothes on?" Gideon chimed in.

"*Ja*. I guess yer right." Eli's face twisted, disappointed, then expectantly, "do ya think I can hold her tamorrow?"

"*Ja,* and try her with the bottle too." Eva smiled at him.

"I can do that. I used ta give lots of *boppli's* their bottles before I came here ta live."

"I expect ya musta been a real *gut* help." Jed nodded and smiled at him encouragingly.

Eli smiled broadly, feeling important.

Jed read the Bible, and Eli made his way up the steps. "Can ya tuck me inta bed, *Mamm*, after ya give the *boppli* her bath?"

"*Ja*, I'll be up as soon as I can," she promised him with a smile and watched him climb the steps. Looking at Jed, "we might need you to hold her over the basin while we wash her hair."

"*Ja*," he consented. "Can ya bundle her in a towel so I can hold her while you an' *Mamm* wash an' rinse her hair?"

"We'll need to wash it at least two times," May

remarked.

"Whatever it takes," Jed nodded.

"Just let me get everything ready before we start." Eva gathered the bathing supplies before removing the soiled nightie she had put on Esther earlier. Bundling the baby proved no problem, but as soon as Jed held her over the basin so Eva and his mother could wash little Esther's hair, she started screaming and squirming. She screamed the whole time the two women rubbed her scalp and scrubbed her hair, hoping to remove some of the accumulated grime and rancid odor.

Jed shook his head at the deafening sound of her screams. Once her hair was washed, he eagerly handed her to Eva while May got fresh water for the bath. Eva rocked and comforted the inconsolable child. Finally, with Esther settled, she sat the baby in the basin of fresh water to bathe her. After the soothing bath, Esther was wrapped in a warm towel, then Eva handed her back to Jed and began drying her hair.

"Now ya know why she never had a proper *gut* scrubbin'," Gideon shook his head and pursed his lips. "If'n she put up that much a ruckus, they probably felt it wasn't worth the trouble."

"Especially when it takes more than one ta get it done," Jed added.

"Well, that won't happen around here," May shook her head in disgust. "I need to rub some coconut oil on her scalp." She looked closely at Esther's head, noticing thick crusty patches, "we need to get rid of that cradle *kappe*."

A half-hour later, Eva braided Esther's hair for the second time that day and pulled a clean nightie over her head.

"What a production." May sat heavily onto one of the chairs at the kitchen table, exhausted. "If she weren't so sickly, we would've never gotten it done."

"She sure is a fighter," Gideon chuckled.

Jed offered the bottle of sweet water, but Esther wanted nothing to do with it and turned her head away.

"Ya can lead a horse ta water, but ya can't make it drink," Gideon commented, using one of his favorite metaphors. Pausing, he turned to his son and asked, "do ya want help ta move the crib inta yer room?"

"*Nee.*" Jed shook his head. "We'll leave it in the room across from us an' leave the door open. That way, if'n she's restless, we can hear her."

"*Gut,*" Eva reached for the baby. "I'll rock her in the rocking chair, and when she goes to sleep, I'll take her upstairs and lay her down."

May rose slowly from the chair. "While you're rocking her, I'll warm up your supper," she remarked while puttering about the kitchen.

Esther slept fitfully that night, with Jed and Eva taking turns checking in on her. Everyone in the Kuepfer homestead suffered from little sleep that night. Even the rooster seemed to have a hard time waking up at four-thirty. Still, Eva counted her blessings as she held onto her little Esther on that new morning.

~ ~ ~

*Defend the weak and the fatherless; uphold the cause
of the poor and the oppressed.*
~ Psalm 82:3 ~

<u>CHAPTER 4</u>
Home Is Where the Heart Is

Eva and May scurried about the kitchen, getting breakfast ready, with Eva making frequent trips to the couch. She offered Esther the bottle and ensured the pillows cocooned her safely so she wouldn't roll off the couch. In fact, she didn't need an excuse or reason to check on Esther; she just went over and talked to her and smiled at her for no other reason than to be a doting mother. Esther sat wide-eyed, giving Eva yet another excuse to go over and cuddle her. "Isn't she the most precious child you've ever seen?" Eva smiled from May to Esther and made sure the baby was covered, so she wouldn't catch a chill, although no one would have thought it chilly in the kitchen with a wood-fire crackling in the cook stove. Eva carried the baby while she set the table and regretted having to set her down to pull the biscuits from the oven. It was surprising how many kitchen chores she could do one-handed, just so that she could keep the baby close to her. But safety preempted her need to mother Esther, and every time she needed to work near the stove, Eva settled Esther into the pillows, peering at her every few seconds to make sure the baby was safe.

"*Ja*," May agreed. "Those eyes tell it all, ain't so?" She went over to tickle Esther under the chin. The older woman voiced an astute observation. "With all that red hair and fair skin, we'll have to watch she doesn't get a rash from the *windel*."

Eva looked over at the couch, alarmed. "You don't suppose she has one already, do you?"

"Did you notice any redness on her bottom when you changed her earlier?" May asked.

"*Nee*. I guess I'm just a little anxious," Eva admitted. "Being a new *Mamm* and all." She smiled sheepishly at May. As an afterthought, she changed the subject, "I need to go to town to get baby cereal, a little cup, and a bowl for Esther. *Ach*, I near forgot; I want to get some material to make her a Prayer *kappe*, a dress, and a smock. Can you think of anything else I should get while I'm in town?" She asked as they continued with the breakfast preparations.

"Why don't you let me go?" May offered. "It isn't a good time to take the *boppli* out. She's still adjusting."

"*Danke*," Eva smiled gratefully at May. "We can pull a list together before you go."

"One thing for certain. All kinds of things will be needed now we have a *boppli* in the *haus*, again." May's words were interrupted by the clatter of the men's boots on the wooden porch as they kicked them off, followed by each one filing into the kitchen to wash up. It was the unspoken cue for the women to concentrate on the unfinished breakfast. Eva took one more look at Esther to ensure she was safely tucked on the couch and turned back to stir the oatmeal.

"Where's Esther?" Eli asked, craning his neck to look around the room.

Eva turned startled eyes toward the couch and let out a sigh of relief. "She's keeping an eye on us," Eva smiled toward the baby.

"Can I give her the bottle?" Eli asked eagerly with anticipation.

"*Ja*, go ahead and give it a try." She looked at Jed, "would you mind helping him while I finish the breakfast? I tried her a few minutes ago, but she kept turning her head away." Eva placed bowls of steaming oatmeal on the table.

Eli snatched the bottle of sweet water from the counter and hurried toward the couch.

"Sit in the rocker *sohn,* an' I'll put her on yer lap," Jed instructed as he finished drying his hands.

Eli readily obeyed, retracing his footsteps to sit in the rocking chair. He eagerly watched as Jed rubbed Esther's back, then carefully picked her up and set her on Eli's lap. "Just rock her a little before tryin' her with the bottle," he advised.

Eli rocked the baby gently. "Why do ya suppose she just looks as if'n she ain't lookin' at anythin'?" He tried unsuccessfully to make eye contact with Esther.

"I expect she's sad," his grandfather offered in the way of an explanation. "She hasn't had anyone wantin' her or takin' the time ta bother with her, an' even though she's a *boppli*, she knows."

"*Ja*, it's goin' ta take all of us ta show her she's special," Eva agreed, walking over to the rocking chair. "Just let her see the bottle, Eli. If she doesn't want it, there's no sense trying to make her take it."

Eli held the bottle for Esther to see, but she turned her head away.

"*Kumme sohn*, it's time ta eat." Jed lifted Esther out of Eli's hold, cradling her easily in his left arm while silent prayer was offered for the food on the table. Jed ended the prayer with "Amen" and handed the plates of food to his dad. When the food dishes came his way again, Jed began loading his plate with eggs, home fries, and biscuits. They casually talked of the different chores needing their immediate attention and tasks that could wait for another day.

"*Dat*, look!" Eli suddenly spouted excitedly, his mouth full of food while pointing toward Esther. Jed's eyebrows raised, ready to reprimand Eli for talking with his mouth full. Eli gulped down the food and blurted, "every time ya put somethin' in yer mouth, she watches an' opens her mouth too!"

Everyone paused, spoons halfway from their oatmeal bowls to their mouths, and watched the baby intently. As Jed raised his spoon to his mouth, sure enough, Esther opened hers.

Eva jumped up from the table. "Go ahead and keep eating, and I'll make her some rice cereal with egg mashed in it. I wasn't expecting her to be interested in food, especially when she wasn't showing any interest in the bottle." She quickly dumped some baby cereal in hot water and poached an egg in another saucepan. Within minutes a bowl and a small spoon were set to the right of Jed's plate. He placed a small amount of the concoction in Esther's gaping mouth and made sure she swallowed it before concentrating on his food.

"Like a baby bird, only without the chirping," May observed with an amused smile.

With each mouthful of his food, Jed glanced down at Esther. When she opened her mouth, he gave her more of the cereal with egg.

"Careful ya don't overfeed her, or she'll upchuck all over ya," his dad warned.

"*Ja*. We want it ta stay down an' get some meat on yer bones. Don't we?" Jed smiled down at Esther, then lifted her and placed her over his shoulder.

"Best put a towel under her head before you burp her," May suggested. "Or she'll be spitting up all over your shirt."

"*Danke, Mamm*. We're kinda new at this," Jed smiled with Eva while rubbing and patting Esther's back. Within seconds a long burp rolled out of her tiny mouth.

"I'd say it's *gut* ta get that up; otherwise, she'd be *krank* an' end up with colic," Gideon nodded.

"Can I try her with the bottle before we go back outside?" Eli looked hopefully at his dad.

"*Ja*, she just might drink somethin' after eatin'," Jed stood up from the table and settled the baby on Eli's lap.

Eli showed Esther the bottle, and she reached for it. "She's sure thirsty," Eli smiled.

"Not too fast, Eli. We need to keep what's in there, down," May warned her grandson.

Eli abruptly pulled the nipple from the baby's mouth and laughed when her mouth immediately turned down, a telltale precursor to crying.

"She didn't much like that," Eva chuckled, keeping an eye on Eli's attempts at nurturing.

"At least she's showin' some emotion," Gideon commented. "Best try burpin' her again," he advised Eli.

Eli placed the baby on his shoulder like he'd seen his dad do and gently rubbed her back. A long belch rumbled up from her stomach, causing everyone to chuckle.

"I'd say he's a natural," Gideon smiled at Eli.

"*Ja*. Natural or not, we best get back ta the barn," Jed headed for the porch door.

Eva lifted Esther from Eli's lap and placed her over her shoulder. "I'll rock her a little. When she falls asleep, I'll lay her on the couch where we can keep an eye on her while we work in the kitchen."

"*Gut* idea," Jed nodded. Touched, he watched Eva's natural maternal instincts where the baby was concerned.

When Eli first came, the boy had only taken to her mothering for so long. And when the space and fresh air of the outdoors beckoned, Eli hurried to join the men doing outside chores, making frequent trips to the house to ensure his new mom and grandmother were still there. They gave him cuddles and cookies to take with him when he left the coziness of the kitchen and the women who loved him unconditionally.

"I need to pick up a few things in town," May looked questioningly at Gideon. "Would you drive me into town later?"

"Fer sure an' fer certain," Gideon nodded. "Is about nine *gut* enough?"

"*Ja, das gut. Danke,*" May smiled briefly before turning to put the kitchen in order.

The men filed out of the kitchen, and Eva finally got a chance to rock Esther. Ten minutes later, she whispered to May, "is she sleeping?"

The older woman peered at the baby and whispered back with a smile, "*Ja*, she's sleeping."

Carefully, Eva slowly stood upright, walked over to the couch, laid the sleeping child down, and propped a pillow against her to prevent her from rolling off.

"She'll have a *gut* sleep now she has some food in her stomach," May commented. The two women went about their chores, washing dishes, making bread, and beginning lunch preparations. Eva alternated checking on Esther and ensuring the pillows were in place with the kitchen chores.

True to his word, Gideon pulled their driver up to the house at nine. Armed with a long list of needed items, May pulled her bonnet over her Prayer *kappe*, left the kitchen, and climbed up to the buggy seat. "We'll be back before lunch," she smiled at Eva and settled back against the buggy seat. "Take *gut* care of our girl."

Eva returned May's smile, nodded in acknowledgment, and turned back into the kitchen to slip over and peer at Esther. 'Little one,' she sighed happily. 'You are as close to having my own *boppli* as I'll ever get.' She smiled tenderly down at the sleeping baby.

~.~.~.~

Eva and Jed had never been blessed with having children of their own. In the five years, they had been married, they tried without success to get pregnant. As one month slid by and then another, no children seemed to be a part of their future. The despair they knew turned to bitterness within Eva's heart - so much so that she lost all hope of ever having a baby. She often wept and, in her despair, pleaded with God, "why have You blessed others with *kinder* but not us?"

In her hopelessness, Eva confided in her friend Miriam, who was full of encouragement. Miriam told her of a friend that knew of a friend who had adopted a child. Eva's hopes were renewed, but when she asked Jed about the option of adopting a child, he wasn't keen on the idea at all. In fact, he was dead set against opening his heart and their home to an English child, an outsider – a child not his own. Eva poured her aching heart out to her friend and neighbor. Of course, Miriam shared with her husband, Tobiah. Tobiah being Tobiah helped Jed realize that giving a child of unfortunate circumstances a home was in keeping with God's will. He pointed out, "It even says, right in *Gott's* word:

...Truly I tell you, whatever you did for one of the least of these brothers and sisters of mine, you did it for Me"
~ Matthew 25:40 ~"

Eva prayed, petitioning God continually, baring her heart and soul, asking God to soften Jed's heart. Then, one evening as they were preparing for bed – out of the blue, he remarked, "We should get in touch with Social Services in St. Thomas. I expect that's the closest place ta talk ta a case worker about givin' a child a home."

A slow, tentative smile crept across Eva's face, erasing the perpetual frown that was beginning to leave permanent frown lines on her face, aging her before her time. "Do you really mean it, Jed? You wouldn't just say that to give me hope, would you?"

Jed laughed. "*Nee,* I wouldn't just say it if'n I didn't mean it," he reassured her.

Eva threw her arms about his neck. "*Ach, Danke, Danke, Danke!* It's really true then. Where do we start?

You don't suppose they'll think we're to *alt,* do you? *Ach,* I can hardly wait until tomorrow to tell Miriam! *Ach, ja,* and your parents! Just think, they're going to have an *enkel* to spoil." Her eyes danced with excitement.

Jed laughed at her enthusiasm, picked her up, and set her on the bed. "Maybe I shouldn't have said anything until tamorrow. It's plain ta see yer goin' ta be too excited ta sleep."

Eva ignored him and prattled on excitedly. "We have to get a bedroom ready. Do you suppose we will get a *boppli* or an older child? Maybe we should get a crib ready and a single bed so we'll be ready. What do you think?" She smiled and then, without warning, began crying.

Jed, kind stoic Jed, rubbed her back and offered the only comfort he could think. "*Kumme,* we should pray an' *Danke Gott* in advance for the *kinder* He will send us."

Eva nodded, blew her nose, gave a long trembling sigh of hopeful contentment, and held Jed's hands as he prayed for them and the child God would send them.

****

The home studies conducted by Social Services and the numerous interviews with family members and friends led Eva and Jed steadily closer to their own child. Although Jed may have been overwhelmed by the multiple appointments set up by Social Services, he carefully hid his impatience, especially when he saw how Eva blossomed. She knew each step carried them closer to having their own child. Eventually, each step led to yet another and, finally, a young boy. He was the only survivor of a house fire in a western county off Lake Ontario and was looking for a permanent home.

The authorities diligently searched central and southern Ontario, as did Social Service workers in Etobicoke, but they could find no living relatives of the little boy. So, young Riccardo Perrico, known by Butch in his neighborhood, was placed on the list of eligible children for adoption.

The transition had not been easy for Butch, then five years of age. Out of necessity, he had been forced to fend for himself. He was one of seven children living in an Italian neighborhood's rough, poorer section. Butch was the scapegoat for his older siblings and a built-in babysitter for his younger two. There was one reason, and one reason only, why young Butch had not succumbed to smoke inhalation, as had his siblings - the older children had beds to sleep in, while his two younger brothers slept curled together in the same crib. He, by necessity, had been forced to sleep anyplace he could find a spot to lay his tired head. He slept on the couch or in a bed with someone else most nights. The night of the fire had been hot, oppressively so, so he had sought the coolest place available, on the porch, stretched out with the neighboring spaniel to keep him company. The Fire Marshall investigating the fatal fire reported two causes for the inconsolable flames. An electrical shortage from the overloaded knob and tube wiring prevalent in the older homes in that part of the city had initially started the blaze. It, in turn, was fed by the dry rotted, termite-riddled wood - a bad combination destined to court disaster. The red-hot flames devoured the house so quickly that the Fire Department hadn't arrived soon enough to douse the inferno.

~.~.~.~

Eva prayed now, as she had prayed then, kneeling beside the couch praying over Esther. Her prayer was of thanksgiving for how she and Jed had been blessed with another child. The prayer didn't stop there; she continued by petitioning God's intervention, asking for wisdom and divine help, that Esther's health would improve and do so in a powerful way. 'I place her in Your hands, *Gott*. Please give me the wisdom to know how to care for this little one and raise her to love You.' Finally, she asked, 'Please, heavenly *Vater*, show me how to be a *gut mamm* to her.' Eva blinked back tears as she stood up, gently caressed the cherub-like face, and smiled at the sleeping child. Like all babies, Esther had an angelic peacefulness about her as she slept, and a warmth settled around Eva's heart as she smiled lovingly at the sleeping child.

~ ~ ~

Hope deferred makes the heart sick,
but a longing fulfilled is a tree of life.
~ Proverbs 13:12 ~

CHAPTER 5
It All Begins at Home

"*Mamm*! *Mammi*! *Kumme*! *Schnell*! Hurry!" Eli called while jumping up and down excitedly on the wooden floor of the back porch.

Eva left supper preparations and hurried to Eli on the porch side of the screen door, drying her hands on her apron as she approached him. May followed close on her heels, both alarmed, preparing themselves for the worst, yet not fully expecting what could be wrong. Eli's boisterous actions proved he was more than alright. They threw open the screen door and were confronted by the three men, with broad smiles plastered across their faces. Their happy and self-satisfied expressions directly resulted from the exuberance Eli had brought to their lives two years before.

"What's wrong?" Eva demanded, her heart tripping faster than usual, looking from one to the other. Confusion set in when there was no apparent reason to fabricate her fears.

"Look what we found!" Eli said, barely containing himself with excitement.

"Actually, it was never lost! But we did dig it out of storage over the carriage shed," Gideon corrected Eli.

"*Ja*!" Eli corrected, "look what we dug out of storage over the drive-in-shed." He pulled excitedly at Eva's hand, still jumping up and down with anticipation.

"*Ach*, Jed's high chair." Becoming emotional, May followed Eva onto the porch and caressed the wooden chair lovingly, grime and all. She looked at Jed. "Your *Dawdi*, my *Daed,* made it for you when you were small," the catch in her voice evident.

"*Ach*, it's wonderful," Eva lifted the little tray.

"And it's goin' ta be perfect fer Esther. Ain't so?" Jed glowed.

"*Ja*, I'll clean it up, and she can use it tonight at supper," May started to pick up the little chair to carry it into the house.

"*Mamm*, let me take it ta the pump ta get the worst of the dirt off, then Eli can bring it in fer ya," Jed offered.

"*Ja*." His mother consented hesitantly, then warned, "but don't go soaking it in water, or you'll ruin the wood!"

"I'll keep an eye on them that they don't," Gideon assured, touched that May was pleased with the recovered high chair.

A half-hour later, Eli carried the long-legged chair into the kitchen. "Here it is, *Mammi*! Esther's goin' ta be all growed up sittin' in this chair."

May took the chair, hugging Eli as thanks for bringing it in, and proceeded to clean it thoroughly with vinegar and oil. When all the obvious grime from years in storage was removed, the little chair received a good dousing in lemon oil, letting the oil sit for twenty minutes before polishing it with soft flannel cloths. She buffed the wood to within an inch of its life, finally stepping back. "It's amazing how one little thing can bring back so many memories," she reminisced. Glancing at Eva, she chuckled. "Especially when Jed stood up in the seat, he was little more than a year old and nearly toppled out. He almost landed on his head. He would have, too, except *Daed* was quick to catch him. After that, we put it away for Jed's children. It's unbelievable how time flies. Ain't so?" She ran fingertips lovingly over the walnut wood.

Eva saw the unshed tears in May's eyes and purposefully remained upbeat. "Now we get to use it again. I'm so glad we have it for Esther. Wouldn't it have been nice if your *daed* could see Esther sitting in it?" She gave her mother-in-law a quick hug.

"For sure and for certain." May nodded, blinking away the unshed tears, and set the little chair to the left of Jed's chair, so it was stationed between Eva and Jed's regular sitting arrangement at the long kitchen table.

Eva placed Esther in the high chair at supper and propped her up on either side with pillows. Esther looked around wide-eyed at the other family members. In front of her, Eva had placed a little spoon on the high chair tray. Deep in concentration, Esther reached for the pale green handle. Everyone chuckled at her focused efforts to pick up the spoon. Eventually, Jed took pity on her and placed it in her hand; immediately, she began banging on the wooden tray but promptly stopped at the noise she was creating.

"Shall we bow our heads in thanksgiving? For all things," Jed added and chuckled while placing his hand over Esther's to prevent further banging. Their prayer ended with, "Amen."

Jed handed the potatoes to his dad. When the bowl was handed back, he loaded his plate with mashed potatoes, then placed a spoonful in Esther's little bowl. Eva mashed carrots and set them alongside the potatoes, then added a chopped boiled egg, and a small amount of gravy was poured over everything. Esther looked at the food and opened her mouth, but she began banging the bowl with the spoon when that produced no results. Eva stood beside the chair and dipped the spoon into the food, directing it to her mouth. Esther ate it, but the puckered look on her face caused everyone to laugh at her animated facial expressions. Next, tiny hands happily squished the food, and into her mouth went the food-laden fingers. Horrified at the mess, Eva pressed the spoon back into Esther's hand.

Jed muttered, "I can see where this could prove ta be real interestin'."

"As long as she's eating, don't worry about it too much for now," his mother advised.

"That makes sense. I can wash her up later," Eva agreed and set some of the emptied bowls on the sideboard before taking a seat on the other side of Esther.

"It's a wonder how such a little one can make such a mess," Gideon shook his head and dug into the food on his plate.

Eli interrupted everybody's attempts at helping Esther. "I was thinkin' about somethin'."

"If'n it's business, we can talk after supper," Jed raised his eyebrows meaningfully at Eli while ignoring his mother's advice and stubbornly trying to get Esther to use the spoon.

"*Nee*, it's not business," Eli insisted. "It's family, an' that's why I thought it was a *gut* time ta talk."

Gideon sat back in his chair and crossed his arms, a smirk on his face as he looked at Jed as if to say, 'Okay, *Daed*, let me see how yer goin' ta handle this one.'

Jed looked to Eva for help, but she nodded slightly, deferring the conversation back to him.

"Well, since it ain't business an' it's family, let's hear what ya've been thinkin' about," Jed consented.

Eli smiled and then became serious as he presented his case. "If'n I get my work done in *gut* time, can I *kumme* play with Esther?"

Jed frowned. "How is this a family matter? It seems a little one-sided, ta me."

"*Ja*. It's a family matter, *Dat*, 'cause I need yer say first. Then I ask *Mamm* an' *Mammi* a *gut* time ta *kumme*, maybe when they're busy an' need help lookin' after Esther." "An' then," he took a deep breath and looked over at his grandfather. "I check with *Dawdi* ta see if'n he can do without my help."

"I see," Jed nodded thoughtfully. "We do have one more family member ta take inta consideration."

The other adults looked at him with varying degrees of perplexity, but Eli had it figured out.

"Ya mean Esther?"

"*Ja*." Jed nodded, looking directly at Eli, thinking, 'This better be *gut*.'

"*Ach, Dat* that's easy. Esther benefits the most. I'm goin' ta teach her *Deutsch* an' keep her learnin' *Englisch*. Teacher at school says I can help teach the *kinder Englisch*, so if'n I keep teachin' Esther both, she won't have to learn when she goes ta school."

Gideon had a hard time suppressing a chuckle. "He's got that one figured out, ain't?" He muttered.

Jed nodded his head thoughtfully, looked at the plate in front of him, and glanced up at Eva with a look that clearly said, "Now what?"

Eva smiled and didn't say a word.

Jed looked at his mother, then over at Eva again. "Ya think ten is a *gut* time fer Eli ta look after Esther?"

May wisely suggested, "since it's a family matter, maybe some days will be different than others. Like washday Monday, he could *kumme* in a little earlier than other days."

"*Ja. Das gut,*" Jed nodded. "We'll go day by day then, an' if'n *Dat* an' me can't spare him, like harvestin', he'll have ta stay an' help the men." Jed looked around the table, and everyone nodded their heads in agreement. "Each mornin' at breakfast, we'll decide, an' ya need to abide with the decision. *Ja?*" Jed looked expectantly at Eli.

"*Ja, Dat.* We're family, an' we stick tagether. Ain't so?"

"*Ja. Das* right," Jed nodded with a smile. Throughout their lives, the Kuepfer family continued to make decisions together, that was this Amish family's way, and it all began at home.

In the meantime, Esther watched the others around the table drinking from cups as they talked, but no one seemed to think to offer her a cup. Finally, as if tired of waiting to be offered a drink, she leaned forward, and baby fingers grasped at Jed's cup.

"*Ach, boppli*!" Jed exclaimed and placed his hand securely over the scalding coffee mug.

Eva jumped up from the table. "I'll get her some *milch.*" Within seconds, she placed a small cup of milk on the tray in front of the child.

Esther promptly grasped the cup with both hands and opened her mouth, tipping the cup toward her. The mug was still inches from its destination, so the milk was dumped onto the high chair's tray. Shocked, she promptly let go of the little cup and immediately became drenched in milk. She inhaled a great gasp of air as the cool milk splashed up into her face, and rivers of the white liquid ran down her, soaking her dress.

Everyone stared in shock at Esther's startled look and splayed fingers.

Eva quickly grabbed a towel from the sideboard, dabbed at the milk on Esther's face, wiped her dress and tray, and set the cup upright. Rather than give up, a determined Esther reached for the cup again, and this time, with Eva's help, it reached its destination. She sucked at the few remaining drops of milk, prompting Eva to pour a little more into the cup. This time the cup reached its goal. Milk ran out the corners of her mouth and down her chin, causing her to gasp for air. Eva quickly pulled the cup away from Esther's mouth. Lifting the cup to her mouth was one thing, but pulling it away again, was still an undeveloped skill. In the days that followed, the art of drinking from the cup was something Esther soon learned. In fact, she caught on to it so quickly that she adamantly refused the bottle, saving Eva the trial of weaning her from it.

~.~.~.~

The next day was an off Sunday. For The People of the Aylmer district, it meant visiting or relaxing at home.

The Kuepfer's usually visited with their neighbors across the way, the Yoder's. They had a picnic at the pond adjacent to Yoder's Mill if weather permitted. Eva and May generally helped Miriam keep an eye on her three active toddlers while talking about quilting, canning, and upcoming events. The men usually took advantage of off Sundays to go fishing, catnap beside the pond, and bring home a catch for supper if fortunate enough. But this off Sunday started differently; Eva had Esther to show off to her childhood friend. She and Miriam had gone to school together and now married, lived across the road from one another.

Jed unloaded the blankets and picnic baskets, then reached for Esther while Eva climbed out of the family buggy. In preparation for dressing Esther in traditional Amish apparel, Eva had stayed up late the evening before sewing a little Prayer *kappe* to cover Esther's head, a shift, and a smock.

Tobiah and Miriam, their three little girls in tow, climbed out of their wagon and came to see the newest addition to the Kuepfer family.

"*Ach*, look at all that hair," Miriam came closer, holding their youngest while their middle child clung to her skirts.

Esther clung to Jed and stared at the new faces, looked over at Eva, then the corners of her mouth turned down, and she buried her face into Jed's shirt and started crying.

"Makin' strange," Tobiah commented.

"*Nee*, more like she's afraid she's goin' ta be passed along again," Gideon returned wryly.

Everyone looked at Jed's dad. It wasn't often he had a say, but they were generally well-thought words of wisdom when he did.

Eva lifted Esther from Jed's arms and attempted to soothe her. Miriam amended, "let's go about putting out the picnic fixings, and she'll settle." The women began laying out the blankets under a shade tree.

It seems when one baby begins crying, the others start sympathizing. Sure enough, they soon had one endless circle of ongoing crying infants. Miriam kept busy consoling her little ones as Eva attempted to reassure Esther. Eventually, a hiccupping Esther began tentatively peeking out at the other children. The women spread the picnic lunch on the blankets as soon as the children calmed down.

Everyone enjoyed the different foods the women had prepared, filling themselves beyond satisfaction. Esther refused food and kept peeking at the others from the security of Eva's arms.

Eli finished eating all he could before offering, "I'll hold her, *Mamm*, while ya finish."

"*Danke*, Eli," Eva had difficulty transferring Esther to Eli's waiting arms.

"She reminds me of a picture I saw once of a little monkey holdin' onta his *mamm* fer dear life," Eli commented as he held Esther.

"She's not planning on letting go, is she?" May smiled and shook her head with a chuckle.

"That's 'cause she knows when she's got a *gut* thing goin'," Gideon remarked.

"She'll get used to it," Miriam commented. "She'll have to. Next Sunday is Meeting Sunday, and everyone will want to see her."

"That's quite the color of hair," Tobiah commented. "It's the same deep red as Jed's beard or next thing to it."

That caused Jed and Eva to look at one another, and they began to laugh. Finally, noticing the questioning looks from the other adults, they shared how Eva had mistakenly braided Jed's beard with Esther's hair at the Social Services office. They all chuckled, causing Esther to look up from hiding her face against Eli's shirt. She gave a toothy smile and clasped baby fingers together while kicking her feet.

"Ya think that's funny, do ya?" Jed leaned closer to Esther, and she patted his face, her smile broadening.

"I'd say she's got ya wrapped around her little finger already. Ain't so?" Tobiah guffawed, privately remembering when it had been hard to get Jed even to consider adopting a child.

"Almost looks like she knows what we're sayin'," Jed straightened.

"Don't underestimate little ones. She might not be able ta talk yet, but she knows where she belongs." Gideon smiled at Esther, tickled that she would be carrying the

Kuepfer name.

"Interestin' how she's perked up in little over a day, ain't?" Jed commented.

"Don't underestimate prayer," Eva murmured with a smile.

...in everything by prayer and supplication with thanksgiving let your requests be made known unto God
Philippians 4:6

Six pairs of knowing eyes turned toward her as she continued. "When we brought her home, and she was so sick and not interested in food, I prayed *Gott* would help us, and I placed her in His hands. In just a few hours, she's changed and starting to eat a little. I think *Gott* has special plans for her, and we're the ones to help her reach them."

Everyone nodded because they knew the power of prayer, even young Eli – for he was a direct answer to prayer, the result of Eva's petitions to God.

"*Ja*. Never underestimate the power of the prayer of a *mamm* fer her *kinder*." Gideon nodded slowly and looked at May with a gentle expression. She, in turn, nodded in agreement. "*Ja*. Jed was my answer to prayer," she smiled at her son, then reached out and placed a hand on Esther's head. "She will be a joyful child and grow to love *Gott*," she predicted. May lowered arthritic fingers and stroked Esther's cheek.

Ruthie squirmed in Miriam's arms. Still clinging to her mother's skirts, her sister, Rosie, said, "*Mamma*, I'm thirsty." Effectively disrupting the conversation on the merits of prayer.

"Time ta get the fishin' poles out," Gideon commented and headed to the shade tree. The other men followed, their bellies satisfied and eager to lounge beside the water.

"*Ja*, if'n we're goin' fishin,' we better take a snack and some of *Tante* Miriam's *gut* lemonade," Eli added with a broad hopeful grin.

"Fer sure," Jed agreed.

"First things first," Eva sighed.

"*Ja*, and that's the wants and needs of *kinder* and *mann*," Miriam echoed Eva's sigh, hers with mock exasperation.

They laughed and packed the men a snack with a large jar of lemonade to be carried along with their fishing tackle.

~ ~ ~

And Hannah said ... I am the woman that prayed unto the
LORD.
For this child, I prayed;
and the LORD hath given me my petition which I asked of
Him.
~ 1 Samuel 1:26, 27 ~

CHAPTER 6
Lessons at Home

Monday morning could not come soon enough for Eli. He had already diligently planned the hour he was given with Esther. Carefully he picked her up and set her in the high wooden chair. Esther looked at him, then over at Eva as if questioning what her new brother was doing. Eva smiled reassuringly at the baby and nodded her head before sorting the laundry. Business-like, Eli placed a chair in front of Esther and took her tiny hands in his, gently clapping them together. Esther soon caught on quickly to this new noise-making game but became quiet when Eli began singing in a singsong voice.

> "Pat-a-cake, pat-a-cake
> baker's man, bake a cake
> as fast as you can.
> Roll it an' pull it

An' break it in two.
Bake one fer Esther
and one fer you."

Esther perked up immediately at the mention of her name. Eli was encouraged at her response and sang the song again, carefully pronouncing each word. By the time he repeated it two times, Esther was patting her little hands together gleefully and garbling.

"What on earth is Eli singing to that child that has her babbling so?" May asked while pushing a pair of Jed's freshly laundered work pants through the wringer of the washing machine.

Eva responded as she fed more clothes into the agitator of the washer. "It's a little song, and he's singing it in *Englisch*."

Both women paused in their work to listen to Eli's lesson, just as he started to sing the song in German.

*"Pat-ein-kuchen, pat-ein-kuchen
backer mann, backen ein kuchen
so schnell wie du kannst.
Rollen sie es und ziehen sie es
Und breche es in zwei teile.
Backe eine fer Esther
und eine fer du."*

May chuckled, looking lovingly at her two grandchildren, "Why, that's not *Englisch*, that's *Deutsch! Gut* for him." She smiled and went back to her work.

Moments later, Eli carried Esther over to where Eva was working. "*Mamm,* can ya stop fer a minute?"

"Eli, I have all this work to do. Can't it wait until later," Eva returned shortly?

"It'll only take a second, *Mamm*." Eli undeterred looked at her imploringly.

"*Ja. Schnell,*" she sighed with a hint of resignation and dried her hands on her choring apron.

Eli hoisted Esther further up on his hip and pointed to Eva. "*Das Mamma*." Immediately, the sternness on Eva's face softened.

"*Mamma,*" Eli repeated and pointed again toward Eva. By the time he had repeated it three times, Esther was repeating, "*Ma-Ma*."

Tears sprang to Eva's eyes; she set the wicker basket on the floor and plucked the baby from Eli's arms. "*Ma-Ma,*" Esther repeated and clapped her little hands together.

"*Ja. Das gut,*" Eli happily encouraged, "*Das Mamma*."

Esther kicked her little legs and patted Eva on the face. "*Ma-Ma*."

"It didn't take her long to learn that one," May smiled.

"*Danke* Eli." Eva pulled him in for a quick hug, "You're doing a real *gut* job with your *schwester*."

"*Ja. Danke Mamm*." He reached for Esther so that Eva

could get back to the wash. "*Mamm*, can we *kumme* an' watch ya hang the clothes out?"

"Is this part of her schooling too?" Eva asked with a smile, unwilling to undermine Eli's attempts at teaching Esther.

"*Ja*, she needs ta see what you an' *Mammi* do, 'cause one day she'll be helpin' too. Ain't so?"

"*Ja*, I guess it wouldn't hurt, but keep a close eye on her." She headed out the back door with the basket of wet clothes on her hip while Eli followed closely behind, carrying Esther.

Throughout the night, all everyone heard was Esther babbling and clapping her hands, repeatedly saying, "*Ma-Ma. Ma-Ma.*" When she finally went to sleep, they were all so exhausted they fell asleep too, only to be awakened a few hours later by a baby voice calling, "*Ma-Ma. Ma-Ma.*"

Tuesday, Eli repeated his lesson from the day before with Esther clapping her hands to the old nursery rhyme. After several turns, he began teaching her 'The Three Little Pigs' in English, then he repeated it in German, wiggling each of her tiny toes. With each turn of the new rhyme, the wiggling of her toes, and gentle tickling, Esther giggled uncontrollably.

> This little piggy went
> to market,
> This little piggy stayed home.
> This little piggy had roast beef.

And this little piggy had none.
And this little piggy went
wee, wee, wee all the
way home.

*Das wenig Schweinchen ging
auf den Markt,
Das wenig Schweinchen blieb zu hause.
Das wenig Schweinchen hatte roastbeef.
Und das wenig Schweinchen hatte keine.
Und das wenig Schweinchen ging
wee, wee, wee ganzen Weg
nach haus*

Eva and May stood at the table and watched in awe. In all their wildest dreams, neither woman thought they would ever hear this baby laugh, at least not so soon.

"Is this the *boppli* you brought home five days ago?" May looked at Eva, stunned.

"It's hard to believe, ain't?" Eva shook her head in disbelief. "But then, nothing is impossible with *Gott. Ja?*"

They continued to listen as Eli taught Esther to say, *Dat.* Within moments Esther was babbling, "*Dada. Dada.*"

"Now we really won't get any sleep," Eva sighed in mock exasperation.

"Why's that?" Jed questioned as he and Gideon walked into the kitchen.

"Listen," Eva warned with a big grin.

"There's *Dat*," Eli pointed toward Jed. "*Dat*. Esther, say *Dat*," he pointed again toward Jed.

"*Dada. Dada*," Esther happily clapped baby hands together.

"*Ja. Das gut, das* real gut," Jed grinned from ear to ear, finished drying his hands, and scooped the baby from Eli's arms.

"*Ja*, 'til she's awake most of the *nacht*, again *tanacht*." Gideon chuckled, shaking his head in exaggerated despair.

Esther's repertoire of words by Thursday included: muck for milk, dink for drink, and Eeee for Eli. Gideon absolutely forbade Eli to teach her, *Dawdi*. However, Esther being as brilliant as she was, one day came out with the word "*Dawee*." They all looked at her in surprise, the most surprised being a pleased, *Dawdi*.

The following day Eli was in the kitchen playing with Esther when one of the farm dogs began barking, announcing a visitor.

"I'll see who it is. Don't leave Esther alone in the chair," Eva instructed, putting down her work and going to the front door.

Eli craned his neck to look out the door, curious to see who had come calling.

"I expect it's the visiting nurse," Eva commented absently, removing her choring apron and tucking stray hairs under her Prayer *kappe*.

"I'll go get *Dat*," Eli offered.

"*Nee*, stay where you are. He'll be up as soon as he sees

the *Englischer* vehicle," she went out to welcome the visitor.

"*Guten morgen*," Eva met the woman climbing out of the car.

"Good morning. I'm Nurse Nancy. I've come to visit you and your new baby. To see if you have any questions and see how the baby is making out," the woman smiled.

Any apprehension Eva may have felt melted at the woman's friendly smile. "*Ja*, I'm Eva. *Kumme* into the *haus*. Eli is playing with Esther, so it's a *gut* time, ain't?"

"Then your son has adjusted to the new family member?" Nurse Nancy's smile was filled with relief.

"*Ja*, he has taken it upon himself to teach her *Englisch* and the equivalent in *Deutsch*."

"Good for him," Nancy returned Eva's smile.

They walked along the porch to the front door. "*Ja*, if you stand here for a little, you can watch how *gut* they are together," Eva suggested. Nurse Nancy accepted the invitation and stood on the porch watching the interaction between the two children. "I was told this infant was Failure to Thrive," she looked at Eva, baffled. "Do I have the right place?"

"*Ja*." Eva smiled, pleased, and reassured her. "This is the Kuepfer farm, I'm Eva, and this is Esther and Eli."

"May we go in?" Nancy asked excitedly.

"*Ja, kumme,*" Eva opened the door for the woman to proceed with her.

Esther had been giggling at one of the songs Eli had

been singing, but seeing the strange woman in the house, she looked at Eva, her mouth turned down, and she began to cry. Eli picked her up, and she desperately clung to his shirt.

"She does that when people *kumme* visiting that she doesn't know," Eva explained.

"Don't worry," Nurse Nancy sympathized. "It's common, especially with children that have bonded successfully with their caregivers."

Eva sighed in relief. "I'm glad; I was afraid you might have thought differently."

"Absolutely not," Nancy reassured her.

"Would you like some *kaffee*?" Eva offered.

"A little tea would be nice," Nancy returned. "Do you mind if I put my paperwork on the table?"

"*Nee*, that's fine." Eva heard Jed's boots clomping onto the back porch as he kicked them off. He came in and washed at the sink as Eva made introductions.

"Jed, this is Nurse Nancy. She has *kumme* to visit us and see how Esther is doing."

"*Ja. Das gut*," Jed came further into the room and extended his hand.

Nurse Nancy shook it with one firm shake and smiled. "It's good to meet you, Mr. Kuepfer."

"*Ja*," he nodded and took Esther from Eli when her insistent, "*Dada. Dada,*" and baby hands reached toward him.

"I like that," the nurse smiled. "Beginning to talk too! I

find it hard to believe the reports sent to me and this baby are one and the same.”

“*Ja*, it’s been one-week taday,” Jed nodded, pleased.

More clomping on the back porch announced Gideon’s arrival.

May poured coffee for the two men and set a cup of tea near their visitor.

Esther immediately reached for Jed’s cup.

“I’ll get her something,” Eva jumped up and put some milk in Esther’s little cup. In the meantime, Jed sat Esther in the high chair. As soon as Eva placed the cup on the tray, Esther grabbed it with both hands and raised it to her mouth, Jed steadying it until it reached its destination.

“She has definitely adjusted,” Nancy smiled. “I would have liked to weigh her, but there’s no need in upsetting her. Regardless, I’ll have to weigh her next week.”

“We can do it taday, if’n ya don’t mind *kummin’* ta the barn.” Jed enlightened the visiting nurse, “there’s a scale we weigh the grain on. I can hold Esther an’ get weighed, then get another with just me, an’ subtract one from the other.”

“What an ingenious idea,” Nancy smiled. “That’ll be great, and then I can complete my report for this week. But I’ll need to come once a week for a little while. They weren’t expecting her to bounce out of this; I want to show that the match for this little one was very successful. It is my understanding that you intend to adopt her?”

Eva looked at Jed, and her face went pale.

"*Ja,* we already consider her as our *tochter.* That is why Betsy Ryan called us. She felt it was a *gut* match," Jed looked at Nurse Nancy unflinchingly.

Nancy nodded her head. "Yes, I must say I definitely agree. But this paperwork must be completed no matter how Betsy or I feel. In the end, it will support your case when the petition for adoption is presented."

"*Ja. Das gut,*" Jed nodded his consent.

The whole Kuepfer family and the visiting nurse trekked to the barn a few minutes later. Jed, carrying Esther, led them up to the granary. His dad manned the scale, adding weights until it balanced against Jed and Esther's weight. Then Gideon placed Esther in Eli's arms, and Jed's weight was obtained. The difference between the weights equaled seventeen pounds.

They all watched the nurse record Esther's weight in the thick file.

"Where does she fit on a regular scale compared to other children her age?" Eva asked with interest.

"A good question, and one only a mom would ask," Nancy smiled at Eva. "My records tell me she is twenty-one months of age," she consulted the paperwork she was carrying. "Almost twenty-two months, and given her height, she looks long," the nurse squinted and looked at Esther in Eli's arms. "I'd say she should be nearer the twenty-five-pound range."

"*Ach,* that's not *gut,*" Eva agonized.

"Mrs. Kuepfer, you are not to worry. Just keep doing

what you have been doing, and she'll soon catch up."
Nurse Nancy looked at Eli. "Do something for me, would
you, Eli?"

"*Ja,*" Eli, who had remained silent up to this point,
agreed.

"Push her sleeve up a little, please."

Eli complied, and the nurse reached over and lightly
squeezed the skin on Esther's arm, then lowered her hand
and made a note on the clipboard she was holding. The
skin on the baby's arm returned to normal.

Esther scowled at the strange woman and pulled her
arm away.

"Little Miss Independence," Nurse Nancy laughed.

"Why did ya do that?" Eli asked, verbalizing
everyone's silent query.

"To see if she was dehydrated," Nurse Nancy
explained, "If the skin had stayed up, that's called
'tenting,' it would have meant she was dehydrated. Since it
returned to normal right away, it means she's getting
enough fluids for her body's needs."

Eli nodded his head in understanding while the adults
breathed a sigh of relief.

"Any questions?" Nancy looked from one to the other.
Everyone shook their heads, 'No.'

"I will come about the same time, next Friday. If you
have any concerns before then, just give me a call," she
handed a small white card to Jed. "My number is on there.
Call any time for whatever reason."

Jed nodded and accepted the card. "*Danke*, we will," he assured her.

Eva lifted Esther from Eli's arms, and they walked with the nurse to her car. They watched her get into it and drive down the lane.

"We need ta get some goat's *milch*," Gideon commented. "It has a higher fat content."

"I'll check with Tobiah. Maybe one of his workers has an extra *milchin'* nanny," Jed offered.

"We still need to watch we don't overfeed her," May remarked. "If she gets sick because the diet is too rich, we'll take two steps back to our one forward."

"Maybe we could keep offering her the same food but give her the goat *milch* instead of the regular *milch*," Eva suggested.

"Is that what ya want ta do?" Jed looked at her.

"*Ja*, and maybe make some ice cream; she might like that," Eva added.

"Who wouldn't?" Gideon laughed. "I'll even churn it fer ya."

"I have dibs on the paddles," Eli smiled at his grandfather.

"*Nee*, that's not how it works," Gideon picked up the challenge and chuckled. "The one doin' the churnin' gets ta lick the paddles."

"I'll share," Eli looked at his grandfather hopefully.

"Fair enough," Gideon laughed, and they all returned to the house for lunch.

~ ~ ~

Then were there brought unto Him little children,
that He should put His hands on them, and pray
~ Matthew 19:13 ~

CHAPTER 7
Love at Home

Esther's cheeks became rosy pink and began to fill out more and more; each day, she was nurtured and nourished by every member of the Kuepfer household. Eli's daily lessons became an anticipated event with the joy and laughter they always brought. The baby blossomed under the one-on-one lessons - she sang when Eli sang, clapped hands when he clapped hands, and laughed and giggled her way into everyone's hearts.

One day, just before lunch, Esther babbled and giggled while propped up on the couch. Eva smiled as she and May worked to get lunch ready. "One thing is certain; we know where she is when she's so chatty."

May chuckled and nodded her head in agreement. It had been a long time since there had been a baby in the house, and it warmed her heart.

When Esther began, *"Mama. Mama,"* Eva thought little of it and hurried to slice chicken for sandwiches.

May's gasp caused Eva to lift her head and follow the direction of May's shocked look. They witnessed Esther standing next to the couch, babbling, "*Mama. Mama.*" Eva set down the carving knife and hurried over to scoop Esther up, but Esther attempted to clap her hands before she got there. However, once Esther let go of the couch's support, she promptly sat down and sat down hard. The shock of suddenly sitting on the hardwood floor was evident by the downward turn of her mouth. Realizing she was still off the couch and no harm had come to her, Esther smiled again and began clapping her hands.

"*Kumme*, little one," Eva picked her up and hugged her before setting her in the high chair. Seeing the perplexed frown on Esther's face, Eva quickly fished out a wooden spoon and small pot. Esther's face became wreathed in smiles, and she had a wonderful time banging the little pot with the spoon. Occasionally, she became so vigorous that the spoon hit her on the nose or other parts of her face. Each time she hit herself, she stopped and scowled but returned to banging the pot with renewed determination.

"What's all the noise about?" Jed came into the kitchen after kicking his boots off.

"Esther was trying to walk, so I thought she'd be safer in her chair while we finished lunch." Eva raised her voice so that he could hear her above the din.

Jed raised his eyebrows at that piece of information. After washing at the sink, he went over to the high chair. Esther stopped banging the pot, looked up at him with a toothy grin, clapped her hands together, and began babbling, "*Dada. Dada.*" Jed picked her up and placed her feet on the floor while supporting her by her hands. Esther jumped and giggled and began pulling to walk forward toward Eva. "*Mama. Mama,*" she smiled, flashing her toothy grin again.

"*Ja,* I see you," Eva laughed, making Esther scrunch her face and huff in and out of her nose. "What a funny face," Eva chuckled at the facial expression.

"*Ja,* she is a joyful child. Ain't?" May smiled.

In the days that followed, Esther began walking while holding onto anything she could get her hands on. Every chance Eli got, he walked Esther, and one day she took off on her own, walking in circles, laughing. Sometimes she'd sit down hard and look about shocked, but she would pull herself up and begin going in circles again within seconds.

When Nurse Nancy visited, she was pleasantly surprised. "Mr. and Mrs. Kuepfer, I'm going to write a recommendation that we do not wait the customary waiting period before proceeding with the adoption."

Everyone stopped what they were doing and looked at her, holding their breath while watching her rummage through her briefcase. Nancy smiled, "since the birth mother has revoked all rights, and since Esther has definitely surpassed our expectations since she has been with you, I am going to recommend the adoption be finalized as soon as possible. The sooner, the better. We need to keep this baby in a stable home."

Eva clasped Jed's arm before sitting down heavily on a

chair. "*Ach, danke*," she smiled through tear-filled eyes.

"*Danke*," Jed returned gruffly, his emotions filling his throat to the point that he had difficulty swallowing.

"Yes, since Child Services have already approved you in St. Thomas and Etobicoke, I will sign the letter of recommendation today. Now, we need to have a lawyer finalize the papers, and Esther will be your child. Do you wish to use the same lawyer you had for Eli when you adopted him?"

"*Ja*," Jed nodded and gave the lawyer's name and his address in Aylmer.

"I'll mail these papers to him on Monday since today is Friday, and it's too late today. Don't worry about anything. I'll also get a copy to Betsy Ryan. The lawyer should be in touch with you soon. I may not make the final decision, but I can expedite the process."

Esther clapped her hands together and scrunched up her face at that precise moment.

"You think that's funny, do you, little Miss. Kuepfer? Nancy laughed. "Well, I think you are a very fortunate young lady to have found such a loving home."

Esther sat in her high chair, kicked her feet, and giggled as the rest laughed at her antics.

~.~.~.~

Before long, Esther was walking everywhere in the house. Jed built a safety guard around the wood stove so she wouldn't burn her hands. Eva decided to teach her how to climb up the steps and then come back down them safely. She knew Esther would eventually attempt climbing them anyway, so she felt it wouldn't hurt to show her how to go about it safely. Eli continued talking to her in English and German until she began to say words in both dialects.

The day Esther discovered the dogs, Eva was overly concerned. Buster and Tiny, the farm dogs, had followed the men to the house and sat panting on the porch. Esther spied them, crawled over to the screen door, and patted the screen, chortling and babbling. "I'm afraid they'll bite her if she becomes too rough," Eva frowned.

"I'll watch that she doesn't hurt them," Eli looked hopefully at his mother.

"No time like the present ta see how things go. The dogs are a big part of the farm; she'll *kumme* across them sooner or later," Jed commented as he finished washing his hands. He picked Esther up, went out to the porch, and squatted beside the dogs while holding Esther on his lap. She looked up at him, then at the dogs, patted Tiny's face, then pulled at the dog's long black coat. Esther gabbed away to the dog and non to gently patted her. Curious, she touched the dog's glistening nose. Looking closer into Tiny's mouth and at her panting tongue and teeth, Esther hunched her shoulders, patting her hands together gleefully. All the while, Tiny sat patiently, seeming to enjoy the attention.

Jed stroked the animal on the head. "*Gut hund*," he praised. The dog looked up at him as if smiling in understanding. Esther watching the exchange, imitated Jed's example and patted the dog gently on the head,

"Better *kumme* wash up for lunch," Eva ended the getting acquainted session. Jed scooped Esther up, sat her beside the sink, and washed her hands with soap, rinsing them under the handpump's running water. They got more water all over than they did rinsing away the soap. Esther giggled and patted her hands together, causing the water to splash in every direction.

"When you two finish makin' a mess," Gideon grumbled good-naturedly, "I need ta wash up so's I can eat."

"Best not stand between your *daed* and lunch," May smiled, her eyes twinkling at Jed.

"*Ja, Dat*," Jed mopped up the water around the sink, picked Esther up, and settled her in the highchair. While waiting for everyone to come to the table, Jed instructed Eli, "after lunch, run an' see what mail was left in the box, would ya *sohn*?"

"*Ja, Dat*," Eli nodded but kept his eyes on the food being placed on the table.

"I have some sticky buns and peaches and cream for dessert," his grandmother murmured to him.

"Fer real, *Mammi*? Sticky buns are my favorite."

"Mine too," Gideon interrupted. "An' peaches an'

cream doesn't get much better than that," he smacked his lips in appreciation.

After lunch, Eli dawdled, going down the lane to pick up the mail. He met the two dogs returning home. "Where have you two been? Yer all wet an' muddy. One minute, yer on the porch an' the next yer at the swamp," he scowled at them.

They looked up at him, their tongues lolling out the side of their mouths as they panted, seemingly amused with their antics.

"Ta the swamp? Huh?" He accused as if expecting an answer and shook his head. "Better not get up on *Mamm's* clean porch, or she'll be chasin' after ya with the broom." By this time, he had arrived at the mailbox, reached in, and extracted a bunch of ads and a large beige-colored envelope. "It's here!" He gasped, forgetting the state the dogs were in and what awaited them if they elected to go up on the porch. He sprinted back to the house with the dogs following close on his heels. Eli bound up the steps making such a racket, Eva exclaimed, "What on earth!?" She glanced up from washing the lunch dishes. "I declare, that boy makes more noise the bigger he gets." She shook her head in mock reproof.

Eli burst into the kitchen. "It's here, *Dat*! *Mamm*, *schnell*; it's here!"

Eva dried her hands and watched as Jed carefully opened the large manila envelope, looking over his shoulder and reading the official-looking letter.

"The lawyer wants us ta go next Tuesday fer signin' the papers," Jed reported to everyone.

"But today's Thursday! That doesn't leave much time to finish the dress I was making Esther, and I wanted to make her another Prayer *kappe*! And I need to let Eli's pantlegs down on his going to Meeting pants. He's grown so tall," Eva paused and looked at Jed. "Next Tuesday, for sure?" Shocked, she sat down hard on one of the chairs.

Jed nodded, smiling at her as the news sank in.

"I'll make the Prayer *kappe*," May offered.

"An' Eli an' me can clean the family buggy," Gideon offered.

"It's goin' ta take the whole family, ain't?" Jed grinned. "Ta make our *boppli* ours."

"*Ja*," they all nodded with broad smiles.

Jed replaced the letter in the envelope and put it inside the family Bible they read each night before bed. It was also where he placed all important paperwork so that it could be prayed over. His dad had done the same thing, and now Jed was carrying on with the tradition.

"What say you about this, Esther?" Jed smiled at the toddler.

"*Mama. Mama. Dada*," she clasped her hands together, scrunched up her nose, and gave a wide grin, laughing in the end and patting her hands together.

"*Ja*, I'd say that about says it all," Gideon chuckled and sat back and looked proudly at each family member.

"*Ja*, an' I can take her ta school an' tell everyone she's my *schwester*," Eli announced, puffing out his chest proudly.

"Not for a few years yet," Eva retaliated somewhat sternly at the thought of her little girl growing up so fast.

"Only four years," Gideon reminded them. "Blink, an' she'll be all grown up with her own little ones."

"A few years yet, *Dat*," Jed reminded him.

"We've had her two an' a half months already," Gideon reminded them.

They all looked at him, about to deny his words, but each one mentally did their own timeline and looked at him, shocked.

"You know something else?" Eva smiled at them all.

They all turned their attention toward her, waiting patiently.

"It's Esther's birthday next Tuesday; she'll be two."

"*Ja. Das* right," Jed looked taken aback and pleased all at the same time. "It's a *wunderbar gut* birthday gift, ain't?"

"We could eat out after finishin' with the lawyer," Gideon suggested.

"It'd be a really nice way to remember the special day," May added.

Everyone nodded their heads in agreement, and Jed stood up. "*Gut* family decision, but right now, there's still work waitin' at the barn."

His dad sighed and stood up as well. "I always feel tired

after eatin'," he grumbled, and he made his way to the side porch, Eli following close behind.

"*Dawdi,* when we eat out, I'm goin' ta have ice cream," Eli announced, oblivious to Gideon's lethargy.

"Not if'n I eat it all first," his grandad teased while pulling his boots on.

"Aw, *Dawdi*. Ya can't eat that much ice cream."

"Are ya sure about that?" Their bantering voices faded as they left the side porch.

"Men and their stomachs," May shook her head and chuckled. "Just finished a big meal, and they're already thinking what else they can eat."

"Call me if'n ya need anythin'," Jed offered and went to pull his boots on before following Eli and his dad to the barn.

"I'm going to put Esther down for a nap," Eva squeezed out a washcloth. "If she doesn't get one, she's generally too tired to settle at night, which means we don't get any sleep."

"*Ja,*" May agreed. "While you do that, I'll start on that Prayer *kappe* for her."

"*Danke,*" Eva nodded while washing Esther's hands and face.

~.~.~.~

Tuesday morning dawned bright and crisp, a suitable pre-Fall morning with great promise in store. The men completed the necessary chores and postponed any elective tasks while the women bustled about in the house, putting things to order, baking bread, and planning the evening meal. One would think a three-day trip was being planned instead of the round trip it would take to drive into town, go to family court, sign the necessary paperwork, eat at Esh's Family Restaurant and drive back home. By nine-thirty, the horse was harnessed to the family buggy and waiting, tied to a tree while Jed hurried into the house to wash up and change.

Eli was fussed over. Beneath his nails and behind his ears were inspected. May hugged him for passing the cleanliness check. Everyone had their best go-to-meeting clothes on, and a nose-bag and hay were packed in the family buggy for the horse. Esther sat on Eva's lap in her new outfit, continually squirming, looking about her with interest, excited to be going somewhere.

"Have we got everything?" May asked. "It'd be best to take a moment now, then have to *kumme* back and be late."

"*Ach*, Jed, the papers that came in the mail," Eva gasped.

"*Ach. Ja, Danke.* Eli, run back inta the *haus* and get the Bible," Jed turned in his seat.

Eli was over the side and bounding up the steps before Jed had completed his request.

"Don't get dirty!" Eva called after him.

Within seconds, Eli handed the Bible to his grandfather

and climbed up to sit beside him. He looked at the others and smiled broadly, ensuring everyone was aware of his willingness to be helpful. Gideon nodded his head once, a twinkle in his eye. "*Ja*, we're ready to go now, ain't?"

"*Ja*," Jed nodded and chirped, asking the horse to move forward.

They arrived at the family court in ample time and sat in the vast waiting area for their turn to come. The lawyer, a tall man wearing a dark business suit with a blue tie, arrived ten minutes before the hour. He spoke in a lowered voice, shaking Jed's hand, "good to see you again. You know the routine from adopting Eli." He turned and looked at the boy. "How are you, young man? Grown since I saw you last."

"I'm fine, thank you," Eli returned, articulating in his best possible English.

"Good for you," the lawyer smiled at him. "Is this the toddler?" He turned and looked at Eva and Esther.

"*Ja*," Eva nodded, pleased with Esther's behavior.

"For the court record, what will be her Christian name?"

"Esther," Jed returned.

"Could we add another name?" Eva asked as if inspired.

"As many as you like," the lawyer waited, pen in hand, prepared to jot down additional names.

"May." Eva looked at her mother-in-law, then at Jed.

Jed nodded, moved by the suggestion. "*Ja. Das gut*. It's

my *Mamm's* name. *Das gut Mamm*? He looked at his mother and smiled warmly.

"*Ja. Danke*," May's smile surpassed any of their broadest grins.

"Good," the lawyer made some notes. "Henceforth, her name will be Esther May Kuepfer. Just relax for a few more minutes; I need to submit this paperwork to the court clerk. We'll go in when they call Kuepfer versus Etobicoke Social Services."

"*Danke*," they all nodded in understanding.

No sooner had the lawyer disappeared through a door adjacent to the waiting area than hurried footsteps sounded on the marbled flooring, echoing throughout the vast waiting area.

"*Ach*, look," Eva gasped.

Jed turned, following the direction Eva was looking. "Betsy Ryan!" He smiled and went over to meet her.

"Oh! I'm so glad you haven't gone in yet," Betsy exclaimed, out of breath. "This was one adoption I couldn't miss; I brought all the original paperwork just in case the court felt something was missing." She held her scuffed brown briefcase up for them to see. "Where's the baby? I'd love to see her."

"Over here," Jed directed her toward his family.

"Oh my." Tears filled Betsy's eyes. "I can't believe this is the same child. Please tell me you haven't swapped her out for another child?"

"*Nee*," everyone shook their heads, smiling and

suppressing chuckles.

Betsy sat down beside Eva and looked at Esther. "Hello, sweetheart. You are a beautiful, beautiful baby, and a very lucky baby, too. May I hold her?" Betsy held her hands out to Esther.

Eva was about to say, 'she doesn't go to people she doesn't know,' when Esther shifted forward and went into Betsy's arms.

"Oh, you are such a precious child," Betsy said, "and heavy too. I love your rosy red cheeks."

Esther looked at her and smiled, showing her tiny white teeth. "*Dada*," she looked at Jed and clapped her hands. "*Mama*," she twisted and looked at Eva, then patted Betsy's arm with chubby baby hands.

"Yes, you have a Mama and a Dada," Betsy looked at Eva and Jed. "Thank you so much for believing in this child."

At that point, more footsteps sounded on the great marble slabs.

"Nurse Nancy!" Eli exclaimed.

"Real get tagether," Gideon chuckled, and the clerk's voice calling for "Kuepfer versus Etobicoke Social Services" interrupted any further conversation.

They took a seat in the impressive room of wooden panels, where a female judge officiated.

'Kuepfer versus Social Services of St. Thomas and Etobicoke, please stand," the clerk called.

After the swearing-in, the papers were signed, and

courtroom pictures were taken. The Kuepfers didn't approve of the images being taken, but they knew it was part of the English system, and to verbally disapprove might jeopardize the adoption process. They also knew the photos would be submitted to each social service department and kept on record at the county seat and possibly in the lawyer's file. Once they shook hands with the judge and the lawyer, they joined Betsy in the large vaulted foyer, where Betsy hugged Eva and enthusiastically shook Jed's hand.

"Eli, what a strong-looking young man you have become," she turned and smiled at Eli. "I was hoping to talk to you before they called us in, and I understand you are teaching your sister English and German."

"Yes," Eli stood a little taller, nodded, and returned her smile.

"Next time I see you, you'll be all grown up," Betsy smiled fondly at him.

"Yes," Eli nodded again and kept smiling.

Then Betsy leaned toward Esther. "Happy birthday, little princess."

Esther smiled, showing her baby teeth, and clapped her hands together.

"We're goin' fer a bite ta eat. You an' Nurse Nancy are *willkommen* ta *kumme* if'n ya like," Jed invited.

"Oh, thank you, no," Betsy returned. "I am totally swamped in paperwork, but it's nice to know I can place Esther's file under 'Successful Placement.' Call me if you ever need anything. Lots more children are looking for a loving home," she hinted and whisked away in a flurry of skirts and tapping shoes.

"I can't linger. I'm hurrying to see another client," Nurse Nancy explained. "I'll come by one more time this Friday to complete my report on Esther. After that, I can come anytime you need me, but I have so many clients waiting to be seen. Some, like Esther, can't wait, but I'm pleased to say she is off my priority list or will be, come Friday."

They said their goodbyes, and Esther May Kuepfer and her family went to Esh's Family Restaurant to celebrate her second birthday.

~ ~ ~

For from Him and through Him and for Him are all things.
To Him be the glory forever!
~ Romans 11:36 ~

CHAPTER 8
Safely Home

Each morning, the first hint of frost covering the ground indicated that fall was inevitable. While the Sugar Maple bushes began changing color to vivid golds and reds, everyone clamored to pick Fall apples and place them in cold storage. Women spent hours over wood stoves finishing canning, whereas the men worked steadily at mending silos, preparing them for the corn harvest. Winter was fast approaching, but an abundance of food was stored in the larder, with preserves neatly lining the shelves in the basement of the Kuepfer homestead. Sweet smelling hay, the staple diet fed to the livestock throughout the winter, was stashed to the rafters in the hayloft.

Eli continued to come to the hous every morning to play with Esther so that May and Eva could finish their various duties. Their time was divided between finishing the canning, doing laundry, and any of the one hundred and one chores that needed completing every day. Esther continued to grow under the affections of the entire household. She learned quickly and was never seen without the faceless doll May had sewn and given her on her second birthday. She could be seen holding the doll, rocking it, or trying to feed it. At night, she refused to settle unless the doll was in bed with her - they were inseparable.

One Monday morning, in the busyness of wash day, Eli came to the house later than Eva and May were expecting him. "Sorry, *Mamm*," he apologized. "The calves got out an' *Dawdi* an' *Dat* needed my help ta round them up, an' get them back inta the field before we could fix the fence."

"That's all right," Eva assured him. "Esther has been quiet, and we're almost finished with the wash, anyway."

"*Danke*," Eli sighed with relief, glad he hadn't received a scolding for coming in late. He kicked off his boots, went in to wash up, and began calling Esther. Lately, she had taken to hiding, and when he found her, she'd giggle and think it was hilarious when he tickled her toes or under her chin. Eli spent a full five minutes looking for her, but she wasn't in any of her favorite hiding places. Out to the clothesline, he marched a frown on his young brow. "*Mamm*, I can't find Esther anywhere."

"Did you try upstairs? She's getting pretty *gut* at climbing the stairs," Eva shoved a clothes peg down on the final piece of wash for the morning.

"*Ja*, I'll look," he smiled in anticipation of finding Esther and tickling her toes. He went back into the house, climbed the steps, and began calling for Esther again. He looked under beds and behind doors and, after an additional five minutes, went back down the steps to the kitchen to inform Eva, "*Mamm*, I still can't find her."

Eva looked at Eli, perplexed. "Eli, I have all this ironing to do; you probably just didn't look *gut* enough."

"I'll help him look," May offered, a slight frown of concern marring her brow, and placed the pot of soup on the back of the stove so it wouldn't scorch. Up the steps they went, searched thoroughly in each room and the linen cupboard – still no Esther. "Let's look downstairs in Dawdi's and my room," May suggested. Afterward, they looked in the front sitting room and the bathroom and returned to the kitchen sitting area.

"I didn't find her anywhere either, and she usually starts laughing when we get close," May reported, furrows of deepening concern on her brow.

"I don't understand it," Eva frowned and set the heavy cast iron on the back of the stove. "Eli, *kumme* look under the couch when I lift it." He did - still no Esther.

"I'll look out at the clothesline; maybe she's waiting for us to bring the clothes in," May suggested, full of hope as she went out the back door.

"Maybe she's in the garden. *Kumme* help me look outside," Eva instructed Eli, now becoming worried. All three searched outside and around the house, meeting at the back porch.

"Eli, run and get your *daed*." Eva held a trembling hand

to her throat and looked at May. "I have no idea where else to look. She's so small. surely, she couldn't have gone that far."

"Let's pray. *Gott* knows where she is, and He'll protect her," May closed her eyes. Eva followed her example. They prayed silent prayers, asking God to protect Esther. No sooner had they lifted their heads than Jed and Gideon came striding toward them.

"She couldn't have gotten far," Jed consoled. "Let's look in the *haus* one more time, then around the pastures. When was the last time ya saw her?" He looked from Eva to his mother.

Eva looked at May. "The last time I remember, she was playing with her doll in the kitchen when I took the last load out to hang it on the line."

"How long ago was that?"

May looked at her son. "It would have been a *gut* half hour ago."

They looked through the house once more, then began going in larger and larger circles out from the house.

Eli came running, "*Dat, Mamm*, I found somethin'." He held up a tiny black felt shoe.

"I sewed that onto the doll," May grew pale.

"Where was it *sohn*? Show us where ya found it." Jed asked in earnest, panic beginning to set in.

"Over there, *Dat*, by the drive."

They all looked down the lane.

"*Dat* where are the dogs?" Eli demanded breathlessly.

"Eli, this is no time ta worry about the *hunds*," Jed returned abruptly as he continued looking around, visually searching the farm's perimeters for any sign.

"He might be onta somethin'." Gideon squinted in contemplation at Eli. "She does like them *hunds*."

Jed started calling for the dogs, following each call with a loud, ear-piercing whistle.

They waited motionless, waiting for an answering bark, or at the very least, expecting the dogs to come around the corner of the barn or house. They waited precious moments, and Eli broke the quietness. "I know where they are." Eli looked from one adult to the other.

Everyone turned and looked at him expectantly. They had exhausted their ideas, and all suggestions were welcome at that moment.

"Bout this time, they go ta the swamp every day," Eli pointed across the field. They all stared, shocked, toward the marsh produced by runoff water from the Millpond. Eva would have fallen, but Jed caught her.

"We'll look after Eva; you go," Gideon commanded.

Jed sprinted over the top of the fence and took the shortcut across the field. Eli followed close behind, but the distance between them increased before long.

"*Tochter* ya need ta be strong," Gideon shook Eva. "Get the buggy while I get the horse," he instructed, running to the barn for their driver.

"I'll get some blankets," May called over her shoulder

as she disappeared into the house.

Within minutes, Gideon and Eva were racing out the drive in the buggy.

Jed lept over the last fence surrounding their farm, his pant leg caught on a large wooden splinter, ripping the heavy material and gouging his skin, leaving a deep wound in his thigh. He fell into the ditch, pulled himself up, and continued hobbling toward the marsh. Eli caught up to him about the same time they heard dogs fighting. "Dear heavenly *Vater*, please let her be alright," Jed gasped.

Eli raced ahead, picking up a long stick as he went. Jed could hear Eli screaming at the top of his lungs long before seeing him. Like a little warrior, he was protecting Esther and Tiny, brandishing the stick at a pack of feral dogs as they circled menacingly around them. Buster and a huge golden cur were fighting, standing on their back legs, teeth bared and snarling.

"Go on, get out of here!" Jed hollered, picking up a heavy stick and bringing it down on the nearest animal. The wild dog yelped in pain and melted into the cattails, tail between its legs, followed by the rest of the pack. "Haw! Get outa here," he charged toward Buster and the larger dog. The mongrel let go of Buster, turned, and glared at Jed, refusing to back down. The noise of the buggy coming down the road momentarily distracted the wild dog, and in that space of a second, Jed brought the stick down hard on the animal's back. Turning, the dog snarled, then skulked away, disappearing into the reeds and undergrowth of the marsh. Jed snatched a crying Esther up. She was covered in mud, and welts and cuts covered her little legs. Her Prayer *kappe* was long gone; regardless, she continued to clutch her faceless doll with one hand while clinging to Jed with the other.

"*Gut hunds*," Jed praised both dogs.

"Give her ta me." Gideon lifted Esther from Jed's arms and wrapped her in a blanket. "Yer leg don't look so *gut*. Get in the buggy. Eli an' me can sit in the back," he handed Esther up to Eva. "She'll be all right," he reassured Eva. "Just got the scare of her life."

"Us too," Jed added and drove the horse down the road until he reached an area wide enough to turn the horse and buggy around.

May stoked the fire in the stove and remained in prayer until she heard the buggy being driven over the gravel in the drive. "*Danke*, merciful *Vater*," she hurried to the screen door. What a sight for sore eyes; Esther was covered in mud, the leg on Jed's pants was ripped open, and blood was oozing from a long gash, but mercifully, they were home.

May and Eva washed Esther, her hair, her body, her clothes, and even the faceless doll. Jed showered, but regardless of what he did to stop the bleeding, the gash on his leg continued to bleed.

"Best get some stitches in that," Gideon observed, "or

ya might get an infection. I'll put the driver to the buggy again. Eli, *kumme* give me a hand."

"*Ja, Dawdi.*" Eli hurried to stay up with his grandad. He'd just finished getting out of the tub and donning clean clothes.

Quickly, May folded a clean tea towel and placed it over the gash on Jed's thigh, wrapping it tightly with another towel. "That should hold it until you have it looked at."

Gideon looked in the back door. "Eli an' me will run Jed inta town. Will ya be alright 'til we get back?" He looked from May to Eva.

"*Ja,*" they both nodded.

"Ya best lock the door once we leave, so the little one won't be takin' any more unplanned trips," he advised.

"*Ja,* we'll look after it. Just look after Jed," May looked worriedly from her husband to her son.

"He's in *gut* hands." With that, the men left. Jed hobbled out to the buggy, but the exertion caused the leg to begin bleeding more profusely. By the time he reached the buggy, the dressing May had applied was drenched with blood, and Jed was starting to turn pale.

Eva stood at the door holding Esther, a look akin to dread on her face as May hurried out with a blanket. "Wrap him in this," she helped Gideon bundle Jed up. Jed attempted to smile his thanks through spasms of shivering.

"He's gettin' shocky," Gideon remarked. "It's a *gut* half-hour drive. We best go." He sent the horse down the drive at a fast clip, raced down the road, through the marsh and into town. "When we get ta the clinic, ya run on in an' get someone ta *kumme* help. Ya hear me, Eli?"

"*Ja, Dawdi*." True to his word, Eli jumped out of the buggy before Gideon pulled the horse to a stop before the clinic door. Afterward, he followed the orderlies back outside and walked the horse to cool him down while his grandad went in with his dad.

Much later, Gideon went looking for Eli. "They're sendin' yer *Daed* ta the hospital fer the *nacht*. He's got a nicked artery; that's why it kept bleedin'."

"Can I go see him, *Dawdi*?" Eli's eyes were as huge as saucers.

"Tamorrow. He's sleepin' now while they wait fer the ambulance ta arrive. He'll *kumme* home tamorrow an' you an' me can *kumme* back inta town ta get him. *Ja*?"

"*Ja, Dawdi*," Eli's eyes filled up with tears.

"Ya did a *gut* job taday," Gideon patted his knee. "If'n it wasn't fer ya, we might still be lookin' fer Esther right now."

"*Ja*, but I was real scared, *Dawdi*."

"I think we was all scared. Plenty scared."

"*Gott* looked after Esther, didn't He, *Dawdi*?"

"*Ja*, I'd say He looked after all of us." With that, they drove the rest of the way home in silence.

Jed came home on crutches the next day with strict orders to rest for a week, then return to the clinic to have the stitches removed.

Resting for prolonged periods is tedious for anyone, but it was like being in solitary confinement in prison for a young and active man like Jed. He kept busy, fixing things on his to-do list, but sitting while doing them definitely cramped his style. Jed tried not to be irritable, but calling Tobiah and his neighbors to harvest the corn irked him beyond measure.

Gideon and Eli were becoming increasingly worn out as the week wore on. Even though they only did the necessary chores, it was still a heavy load for a man Gideon's age and a young boy just learning the ropes of running a farm. The evening Eli fell asleep at the supper table was the day Jed put a stop to his enforced rest. "Eva, wash him up an' put him ta bed. An' let him sleep in, in the mornin'. I'll go ta the barn after supper an' help *Daed* finish off fer the *nacht*."

"*Ach*, Jed *nee*. I don't want you to get an infection in your leg," Eva looked at him, concerned.

"I won't. There's still a dressing on it, and I'll be careful not ta get it wet."

"Then I'll *kumme* out and help *Daed* put the horses out and *milch* the *couw*. You can feed the stock."

"*Ja, das gut*," he conceded begrudgingly.

"I'll put the *kinder* to bed and tidy up in the *haus*," May volunteered. "You need to be careful; it's still two days before you go back for a check-up," she looked at her son, concerned.

"*Ja*, I'll be careful," Jed nodded, glad to be doing something constructive again.

An hour later, evening chores done, a pale Jed hobbled on his crutches to the house, flanked by Eva and Gideon. Eva knelt to remove his boots while Gideon went into the house to wash up.

"I'm headed fer bed," Gideon murmured.

"Don't you want a hot drink and pie before going?" May asked, speaking to his retreating back.

"Not ta *nacht*," he muttered and continued wearily to their room on the first floor.

May's forehead drew together in a frown. 'My *mann* refusing food? He must be more tired than I thought.'

Eva came into the kitchen. "Is Esther in bed?"

"*Ja*, I put them both down. They fell asleep as soon as their heads hit the pillow," May assured her. "Where's Jed?"

"Sitting and catching his breath on the back porch."

"How did it go at the barn?"

"We got the chores done, but Jed keeps fretting it's too much work for *Daed* and Eli."

"Tobiah said he'd help. Why don't you go ask if he can spare some time?" May encouraged.

"*Ja*, I'll get Jed settled on the couch and then walk over."

"Let me look after Jed. You go before it gets too dark,"

May prompted.

Eva looked at May and nodded. "*Ja*, maybe you're right. I'll be back as soon as I can. I can't imagine I'll be gone more than fifteen or twenty minutes."

Jed hobbled in from the porch.

"Sit on the couch and put your leg up," May instructed. "I'll get you something to eat before you go to bed."

"I'll be back as soon as I can," Eva quipped as she slipped out the kitchen door.

"Where are ya goin' at this time of the day?" Jed called after her.

"She's going to ask Tobiah if he can help for the next few days," May informed him.

"He can't do that. He has enough work ta do with the mill an' farm ta look after." Jed eased to the edge of the couch to stand up, intending to call Eva back.

"*Ja*, he can. And he will," May informed him assertively, reminding him who the parent was. After a pointed look toward her son, she continued preparing a snack for him. "Do you want your *daed* to have a heart attack, and you get an infection in your leg just because you won't listen?" She gave him a determined look. "You need to listen to me, Jed. We need help, and that's that, so don't go giving me any grief. It's a wonder how you expect me to be patient when your stubbornness is hurting the rest of us. If you won't think about yourself, think about your *daed* and your *sohn*. They'd both drop rather than disappoint you. We can't keep on like this." Her attitude softened, "besides, it'll only be for a few days until you're back on your feet." She looked over at him, half expecting her son to object.

"*Ja, Mamm*," Jed answered resentfully. Thinking, 'it ain't often *Mamm* gets upset, but when she's right, she's right,' he admitted begrudgingly. Giving a deep sigh, he settled back against the cushions on the couch as she had instructed him to do in the first place.

A few minutes later, Eva returned with a broad smile. "Tobiah says it's slow at the mill, and we'd be doing him a favor by keeping a couple of his men busy until his next shipment of logs *kumme* in. He says that should be two weeks from now."

Jed looked at his mother with resignation. "*Ja, das gut*," he nodded, sighing in acceptance.

"It means we'll have a couple more mouths to feed at lunchtime," Eva looked apologetically at May.

May brushed off the extra work. "What's two more when we're already cooking. Besides, it makes an *alt* woman feel useful again, not so much a broken spoke in a wheel. *Ja?*"

"*Ach, Mamm*. You could never be that." Eva looked at her with concern realizing for the first time since coming to live in the house that, first and foremost, it was May's kitchen, May's house, and it was May that had generously opened her home to her.

The following morning, two young men in their early twenties walked over from Yoder's Mill and went straight to work under Gideon's watchful eyes. They repaired threshing equipment, sharpened and oiled the blade on the mower, repaired fences, milked the cow, mucked out pens, and kept busy with all the chores needing to be accomplished on the farm. Having the two young men work on the farm got the to-do list completed and other chores too heavy for the Kuepfer men to complete on their own. Eli worked with them and gained valuable experience from the worker's new perspective.

One of the young men came from an old established dairy farm. With Jed's permission, Eli bought his first Holstein heifer from him. The young man showed Eli how to handle the calf, care for it, and train it for milking.

Ten days after having his wound closed, Jed had the stitches removed. He received a firm warning not to exert himself but to gradually slide back into the rigors of farming. Hobbling around on crutches, he helped his dad supervise chores and remained active in the decision-making around the farm. Often, when Eva took cold drinks to the men, she'd find him in the corner of the drive-in shed, cutting and sanding wood for Adirondack chairs. He had figured out a way to make the chairs glide instead of sitting stationary or rocking, and he was excited about making his ideas a reality.

Esther was never left unsupervised. A special latch was installed high enough on the door that she couldn't reach it. May and Eva often watched as she stared up at the restraining fixture. They exchanged looks and shook their heads. "*Schmart*, real *schmart*," May murmured.

"*Ja*, maybe too *schmart* for her own *gut*." Eva agreed, setting a pot and spoon on the floor or some other object to occupy her young daughter. The hope was that Esther wouldn't continue obsessing over the locked door.

"She needs something to do," May observed.

"I don't know what; she's too young to sew. Maybe we could give her some dough, and she could make a turnover."

"I'll get Gideon to make a small rolling pin, and maybe Jed could make a large blunt-ended wooden needle for her," May pondered. "Meanwhile, I'll make some clothes for her doll, and she can change its clothes. Between them, the two women came up with a collection of ideas to occupy Esther's time. The men got in on the brainstorming as well.

"My *mamm* had my *daed* put up a clothesline my *schwester* could reach, and she hung up the socks and other small things like tea towels and hankies," one of the young men from the Mill contributed. So, a clothesline was stretched between two short poles, just high enough for Esther to reach. On baking days, she was appointed an end of the table, and May helped her roll out pastry. May taught her to set a spoonful of preserves in the center, fold the top over and flute the ends closed. She had her own little choring apron and was given a basin to wash the kitchen utensils she'd used. It was always necessary for either Eva or May to rewash the dishes, but that didn't matter. The fact that Esther was doing something is what counted. She was occupied and happy, which kept her out of trouble for the moment.

~ ~ ~

Be ye all of one mind, having compassion one of another, love as brethren, be pitiful, be courteous
~ 1 Peter 3:8 ~

CHAPTER 9
Instruction at Home

By the time Esther was five years of age, she was as fluent in German and English as a five-year-old could be. Teaching Esther English allowed Eli to keep up with his English, effectively making him well versed in both languages. The summer before Esther turned six, she was so excited about starting school that she constantly talked about it. It became impossible for anyone to talk about anything without Esther bringing up the subject of school. On her first school day, she set off in a business-like fashion, walking smartly beside her big brother. It was an exciting day for Esther but sad for Eva. The baby she had dwelt on and nurtured was beginning to grow up. Eva waved nostalgically at her two children, keeping an eye on the long dark red braids covered by a newly sewn Prayer *kappe*. When Esther and Eli got to the end of the lane, they turned and waved enthusiastically. She returned the wave, wishing she could call them back.

Eva lingered, watching as her children stood at the end of the drive, waiting for Miriam and Tobiah's three girls. 'Is this what an empty nest feels like?' She dabbed at the tears collecting in her eyes as she kept post at the door. Giving a sad sigh, Eva wondered if her long-time friend, Miriam, felt just as miserable as she watched her children leave for school. After one final wave, Eva turned back, took another look through the screen door, and walked into the kitchen. She sighed while her children walked in the opposite direction to the one-room schoolhouse a concession over.

Not long after the new school year had begun, Eva and Jed were visited by Sadie Heffner, the teacher at the one-room Amish schoolhouse. They sat on the porch, rocking and sipping lemonade while sharing generalities.

Finally, full of curiosity, Eva couldn't wait any longer and asked, "How are the *kinder* settling into school?"

"Very well," Sadie smiled and nodded.

Eva returned the smile and sat back in her chair, relieved.

"Perhaps too well," Sadie added with a chuckle.

"How so?" Jed frowned.

"Well, Esther knows *Deutsch* and *Englisch*." Sadie then began rhyming off a long list of Esther's attributes. "She writes her name well, counts, and adds single digit numbers just fine. As well, she can read simple sentences. I just don't know where to put her. She's far ahead of her classmates. The other day, she was helping them with their

Englisch lessons."

Jed and Eva chuckled and said in unison, "That's Eli's doin'."

"How do you feel about putting her ahead a year?" Sadie looked from one to the other, hopefully.

Eva frowned and looked at Jed.

"What are ya thinkin'?" Jed looked evenly at Eva, nodding for her to go ahead.

"I'm not sure that's a *gut* idea." Eva looked from Jed to the teacher. "She hasn't turned six yet, and the *kinder* in the next grade will be seven and eight years old."

"Well, how do you feel if she stays with the group she's in, and I'll introduce more challenging work?" Sadie brainstormed.

"*Ja*, that should work. Just don't go pushin' her on. Knowin' how she figures things out, she'll be the youngest graduatin' student ya have," Jed advised with a chuckle. "She needs a chance ta be with the other *kinder* before pushin' her on ta be an adult."

"She is *schmart*." Sadie nodded her head eagerly yet somewhat exhausted in her attempts to fit Esther Kuepfer in a class where she would be challenged.

"*Ja*, we figured that out a long time back," Eva chuckled, recalling Esther's early years.

Shortly after the impromptu parent-teacher meeting, Sadie said her goodbyes and drove her horse home, deep in thought. She had a lot to think about. 'Esther Kuepfer will be a challenging prospect. *Nee!*' she corrected herself, 'Esther Kuepfer IS a challenging prospect.'

Esther began helping with supper that evening, placing the plates in the warming closet over the stove. She set about her task with a self-righteous, slightly pompous attitude. Exuding an air of self-importance, she announced, "I saw Teacher *kumme* to see you and *Dat*," she smiled broadly at Eva.

"*Ja*, she wanted to tell us how well you were doing at school," Eva admitted.

"I know!" Esther smiled proudly with an imperious attitude. "She thinks I'm *schmart*. That's what I heard her say, that she thinks I'm *schmart*! Ain't so?"

Eva looked at Esther's smug look, then over at May. The two women exchanged a knowing glance. May returned to rolling out pastry dough, taking an exaggerated interest in the chore before her.

"*Ja*. You are *schmart, Tochter*. But with that *schmartness kummes* responsibility; it does not please *Gott* when we brag about the gifts He has given us. You are to use your gifts to help others and therefore glorify Him. Do you know you can lose a gift if it isn't used or used wisely?"

"*Ja, Mamma.*" Esther nodded, her enthusiastic air of importance dampening a little.

"As well, it does not please me that you were eavesdropping on someone else's conversation. An *alt* saying goes, 'eavesdroppers never hear anything *gut* of themselves.' You're not better than anyone else, just because you're *schmart*. You're *schmart* because of everyone else." Eva paused, looking at Esther's crestfallen face. "Don't forget the times Eli spent with you, playing games so you would understand *Deutsch* and *Englisch*. And your *Daed*? Along with *Dawdi,* help all the time. They are strong, *Gott*-filled leaders of our home. *Mammi* and I show you how to sew and help in the kitchen preparing meals," Eva looked at Esther with concern, hoping her daughter understood what she was saying.

"I didn't know," Esther shook her head, her eyes brimming with tears as she looked down at the floor.

May intervened and offered in her gentle way, the Bible says:

> *Every gut and perfect gift is from above,*
> *kumming down from the Vater of lights...*
> *~ James 1:17 ~*

"I'm sorry, *Mamma*. I won't listen to what others are saying anymore. And I'll try not to forget how everybody helped me." Esther's look of sadness completely replaced her previous air of arrogance.

"*Gott* loans us gifts for a season. It's what we do with them that counts," Eva concluded, smiling kindly at Esther, disheartened that she had to chastise her daughter. Giving her a warm hug, she encouraged, "*Kumme*. The men will be in for supper soon. Help me get these carrots ready. You can drizzle some honey over them while I add a little salt and pepper, then we'll put them in the oven to cook."

"*Ja Mamma,*" Esther nodded, deep in thought. She happily helped with the carrots and then placed the cutlery on the table for supper. In the years that followed, she became a deep thinker, always active but very careful with her choice of words, not wanting to offend others by speaking meanly or out of turn.

~ ~ ~

Whoever exalts himself shall be humbled;
and whoever humbles himself shall be exalted
~ Matthew 23:12 ~

CHAPTER 10
Education at Home

Like all Amish children, when Esther graduated from grade eight at age thirteen, her education changed from classroom academics to learning to run an Amish home. It is common in Esther's peer group in the Amish community to take on part-time work; many use that income to save for starting a business, purchasing a farm, or building a hope chest or dowry. Unfortunately, Esther was too young to take a job at The Market, or the restaurant in town, so Eva decided they should make quilts and pot holders to sell at the Wednesday Farmer's Market. During the summer, they also sold surplus garden products at the vegetable stand Jed had built and set up at the end of the drive.

Every second Sunday, the family attended Meetings. Esther was excited to catch up on any news with her former classmates, especially her best friend, Hannah. Hannah always had a lot to share about the joys and challenges of working as a mother's helper. There was always an abundance of stories to tell while replenishing the food tables and washing dishes. Both girls cherished the opportunity to compare notes.

The year they turned sixteen, Esther and Hannah looked forward to finally getting to attend the Saturday night singings. Eli had been going to the get-togethers for the past five years and willingly offered to drive them to the singings and safely escort them home afterward. It was a perfect arrangement until he began showing an interest in Naomi Woerner and taking her home after the singings. That was problematic because Esther and Hannah had no ride on the return trip home. To the girls' overwhelming relief, their fathers took turns volunteering as chaperoning adults. Unhindered by transportation worries, it gave them a chance to mingle with the others, sing, play games, and eat before the evening came to a close.

Shortly after Esther and Hannah began attending the singings, a young man in his early twenties moved into their district and attended the gatherings. Frequently, young men moved from other communities where jobs weren't as plentiful to find work. Thomas Jantzi came from Lucknow and was looking to learn a trade. Until he settled onto a chosen occupation, he bartered for food and lodging in exchange for work on the surrounding farms around Aylmer.

Before long, Thomas began offering some of the girls rides home after the singing. It was never the same girl twice in a row, that is, until the evening he met Esther. Perhaps it was because Esther was pleasant to be around, or maybe it was her brilliant smile. He enjoyed that she carried the conversation, and he didn't have to respond except to nod his head or respond in some other noncommittal way. His interest in Esther became evident to the whole community each time he drove her home after the gatherings.

When Jed told her of the newcomer's sudden interest in their daughter, Eva was horrified. "She's too young," she protested to Jed. "He must be six or seven years older than she is!"

Jed returned Eva's accusations with a perplexed sigh. He was just as concerned as Eva, but how to handle the matter without pushing Esther away from them right into the young man's arms. "We brought Esther up with wisdom an' intelligence. Let's leave it ta *Gott's* leading an' trust that everythin' will work out as it's intended ta."

In the meantime, Hannah had convinced her parents to let her go on *rumspringa*. The next time Esther saw her friend, Hannah was bursting at the seams with excitement. She was full of ideas about spending her time away from the Amish community. Esther got caught up in the moment of excitement and was convinced she should go along with her friend.

Eva paced the kitchen floor beside herself. "One option over the other – marriage opposed to *rumspringa*! What a choice!" She fussed at Jed.

"Look at it this way," Jed tried to console her. "If'n she goes with Hannah, they will have one another, an' they'll *kumme* home in nine ta ten months. If'n she stays, she'll marry Thomas, an' a year after that will have a *boppli*. Her life will be all mapped out fer her, an' we'll have little say in it once she marries." Jed shrugged resignedly. "The way I see it, chances are Thomas will get tired of waitin' fer her an' will have moved on – hopefully back home."

Eva closed her eyes, 'Dear heavenly *Vater*, what shall I do?' Instantly she knew what she must do – against all odds. She approached Esther, "I think you and Hannah should apply to go to Fanshawe College, just north of here in London. I know for certain they have a *gut* small business course. It wouldn't hurt you, and Hannah either, to go for a year and learn how to *markt* and sell the quilts we make. I have a friend who lives in London's south end, and you could live with her."

"How far is that away from the College, *Mamma*?" Esther's interest was piqued, especially at her mother's sudden change of heart.

"Nine miles at the very most to the University of Western Ontario or Fanshawe College. They're both at the north end of the city. You could take the city bus, and students get a special fare."

Hannah's parents were excited over the prospect of the girls spending *rumspringa* together. The girls would have one another, giving them a chance to see how the English world functioned. But much needed to be accomplished before enrolling at the college; the most significant hurdle would be to prepare to write their GED equivalency tests.

First, they headed to the library to find out where they would need to go to study before writing the tests. Fate must have been smiling down on them. The library had just begun hosting study classes supervised by local secondary school teachers.

Esther and Hannah always made it a point to study together, which, as it happened, was a good thing. Esther's strong points were math and sciences, while Hannah excelled in grammar and literature and seemed to have a knack for memorizing the dates in history. Following an intense period of study and preparation, the girls wrote the entrance exams the summer before they turned seventeen, passed, and were accepted as freshmen at the college. It was an understatement to say preparing for college was overwhelming, but it didn't end there. Not only would the girls be rubbing shoulders daily with non-Amish students, but they would be surrounded by others experimenting with 'the party scene.' It would be a time for them to live in the English world and weigh their conservative lifestyle against the more boisterous lifestyle of the other students.

While Esther and Hannah were preparing to stretch their wings, Eva did her part to ensure her baby was safe. She wrote to her friend, Julia, explaining the girls needed a place of lodging and, more so, someone to oversee their activities. Julia wrote back to say how happy she was to take the two girls under her wings. She even volunteered to take them to the college on registration day and then stand with them in the long line-ups to purchase their textbooks. When orientation day arrived, Julia made sure they participated, so they would know where the classrooms and administration offices were located. With heads crammed full and folders filled with paperwork and maps, Esther and Hannah's active imaginations began wondering what basic computers, economics, accounting, marketing, and business management involved. Exhausted but exhilarated, the two girls returned to their home away from home. Julia placed bowls of nutritious homemade vegetable soup and grilled cheese sandwiches on the table for them, listening to their excited chatter about the next day of classroom instruction. She interrupted them late into the evening, reminding them that morning came early, and the city buses were on a schedule and wouldn't wait for them. Naturally, both girls slept very little that night. They talked in subdued voices into the wee hours of the morning and excitedly mapped out their plans, hoping to go home every second weekend. They looked forward to spending time with their families and returning loaded with home-baked goodies. Finally, when sleep did come, morning came fast on its heels, and both girls, full of youth, bounced out of bed excited to be attending their first day of college.

Meanwhile, Eva and Jed were not satisfied with the turn of events between Esther and Thomas. Esther had left on *rumspringa* with a promise from Thomas that he would wait for her while she was away. "What's another year?" On their final drive home from the Saturday night singing,

he had shrugged. Esther was beside herself with
excitement. She was going away on *rumspringa* with her
best friend Hannah, and Thomas had promised to wait for
her - what more could a sixteen, going on seventeen-year-
old girl hope for? In her estimation, life was perfect! Her
future seemed flawless and rosy; she had it that well
planned. Whatever could go wrong?

~ ~ ~

A man's heart deviseth his way:
But the LORD directeth his steps.
~ Proverbs 16:9 ~

CHAPTER 11
A Home for Eli

The routine in the Kuepfer household remained the same while Esther was at college, a little more than an hour's drive away. There was one exception; it was evident from the gleam in Eva's eyes that her baby was coming back home every two weeks. Starting on the Thursday before Esther's arrival, Eva was in the kitchen baking up a storm, preparing all of Esther's favorite meals.

The family, especially Eli, waited for Esther's weekend visits and the news she would share of her adventures at school. As it turned out, he soon had some news of his own, to share with his sister.

Eli was twenty-two, strikingly handsome with his inky black hair and deeply tanned complexion. In his willingness to apply himself and work hard, he had already started a small dairy herd in hopes of one day having a large dairy production. He did realize one thing – the home farm would never be big enough to support the future he envisioned.

It was almost as if Jed was privy to Eli's inner thoughts. "It's 'bout time we looked fer a farm fer ya," Jed announced. "One day yer goin' ta want ta get married, an' start a family. It'd be best ta get yerself situated first."

Eli's embarrassment deepened his coloring to a robust swarthiness, but he nodded in agreement. He knew his dad was right. If he ever hoped to move on with his friendship with Naomi, other than buggy rides at night, it was time to move forward with his plans.

Jed ignored his son's red face and continued, "I hear there's a nice farm over a couple of lines that might be fer sale. It's been let go, but the buildin' has some *gut* bones. We can get the lumber from Tobiah cheap an' fix it up – a little here an' a little there. If'n yer interested, we could ask Tobiah ta go with us an' have a look-see."

Two days later, the familiar site of Tobiah's draft pair hitched to his wagon was seen pulling into an old, dilapidated property. Tobiah had been honored and more than ready when Eli asked him to join them when inspecting the property. When the three men drove up the lane, the elderly English man who owned and lived in the house came to meet them. The men introduced themselves. "We were wonderin' if'n ya still might be interested in sellin' yer farm?" Jed asked.

The older man scratched his head. "What are ya lookin' ta do with it?"

Eli interjected, seeing hope in the situation. "I have a small herd of Holstein, an' I want ta set up a *milchin'* operation."

"Yer not interested in subdividin' an' sellin' off prime farmland ta put a bunch of houses on it, are ya?" The older man squinted, looking at him closely.

Eli smiled and shook his head. "*Nee*. I want ta farm an' yer place looks just the right size. I was wonderin' if'n ya'd be interested in sellin' it an' how much ya'd want?"

"Ya know what ya want, don't ya boy? I like that. Well, I'll tell ya what some developers have offered me, an' if ya can come anywhere close, I'd say we have a deal. Except," the old man paused. "I do have one request."

"*Ja?*" Eli's interest rose, wondering what his request would be.

"I want ta stay here 'til it's time fer me ta check outa life, as we know it, anyway. There's a little summer kitchen at the back of the house. I'll sell it to ya as long as I can stay in those rooms at the back of the house."

"*Ja. Das gut,*" Eli nodded slowly, thoughtfully. "How much are ya askin' fer it?"

"Mind, it's prime land." The old man defended his following words, looked at Eli skeptically, and added, "There's a lot of work needin' done. I just haven't had the energy or interest since my wife passed on." After a moment of working his jaw and rubbing his chin, he named his price.

Eli bit his bottom lip, nodded thoughtfully, and mentally weighed the pros and cons.

"I'd say it's more than a fair price," Jed murmured to Eli.

Eli looked over at Tobiah and raised a questioning eyebrow. Tobiah returned the raised eyebrow with one of his own and gave a curt nod of approval.

Eli smiled and offered his hand to the other man. "We have a deal. I'm Eli Kuepfer."

"Just call me Pops," the old man shook his hand vigorously. For an older man, he had a good grip.

"Can we have a look see in the *haus* an' then the barn?" Eli asked.

"Sure, come on in. It's not as clean as when my wife was alive but come on in, anyway." He led the way through an overgrown garden and gave them the grand house tour.

"Now we've seen the main part of the *haus*, I want ta see the area ya'd like ta live in," Eli looked at Pops expectantly.

"Just through this here door," the old man indicated with a nod. He led them down a hall with wainscoting on the lower half of the wall and wallpaper on the upper half and opened a paint-chipped door to reveal a spacious area. The sun flooded through the windows and glass in the lone door leading outside. Two inside doors led off the large room to two smaller rooms. They looked around. "There's no bathroom," Tobiah noted. "But we could convert the smaller room over ta one, and later it'd make a *gut Dawdi haus*."

Eli and Jed nodded in agreement.

Eli turned to Pops. "Why don't ya go ahead an' stay in the main *haus*, an' we'll get these rooms ready fer ya ta live in, then ya can move back here while we paint in the main part."

"You'd do that for me?" Pops looked relieved.

"*Ja*, if'n you're sellin' me the *haus*, I plan ta do some work on it before I move in, an' I want ta make sure the insulation is up ta code an' that the pipes will stand up ta the cold winters."

"What's the basement like?" Tobiah asked.

"It used to be a good dry basement, but the last few years, it gets damp in the spring following the melt."

They all filed downstairs to the basement. Pops was right; it did smell of dampness.

"We'll dig around the foundation, put up a moisture barrier, make sure the eaves troughin' is cleaned out, an' the downspouts are carryin' the water away." Tobiah continued to inspect the old stone foundation. "It looks solid," he concluded.

"The barn's not in too good a shape. I haven't been out there in years," Pops informed them, and they made their way to the enormous hipped-roof barn.

"The steel on the roof needs fixin'," Jed looked up at the massive holes in the roof where a strong wind or consecutive winds had peeled the roofing away. They looked inside, without actually going in, just in case the wooden loft floor was rotten. The old hay was musty and damp from the latest series of rainstorms, and one of the enormous sliding double doors was hanging precariously from one trolley.

"Let's look downstairs," Eli suggested, hoping it was in better shape. They went down the gangway and tried to open the door to the stable area in the lower part of the barn.

"Swollen from the rains," Jed surmised.

"We can get in a back way," Pops set out in a hobbling gait.

Sure enough, the door on the south side of the building swung open with a deep squall emitting from its hinges. Tobiah looked up at the overhead flooring. "Just what I was hopin'. The hay has preserved the wood in the loft floorin' from rottin'."

"We best tackle the barn first before it gets worse," Eli mused.

"*Ja*, then the back of the *haus* fer Pops ta live inta. But I agree. It'd be a shame ta lose the barn. Probably cost more ta rebuild than salvage. Still, it ain't goin' ta be cheap. I know where we can get the lumber an' the help, cheap enough," Tobiah laughed at his own joke. "But the steel fer the roof is goin' ta be expensive. I can get it wholesale fer ya. Let's look outside again an' see how much we'll need." So out they went to inspect the roof again. "Probably fifty, twelve-foot sheets, an' if'n ya don't need it all fer the barn, ya can keep it for the outside sheds,"

Tobiah suggested, indicating the sorry buildings that might house farm equipment.

Eli turned to Pops. "I'll set up an appointment with the lawyer in town, an' we can exchange the deed fer yer askin' price."

"Does it matter who we use for a lawyer?" Pops asked; his beady brown eyes challenged Eli.

Eli looked at his dad. "I suppose not," Jed returned.

"That's good, 'cause I can go into the house and call my lawyer, and he'll fit me in right away."

Eli shrugged. "Sounds gut ta me." So back to the house they headed.

Pops looked the phone number up in an old dog-eared phonebook and asked to speak with his lawyer. "Not in ya say?" Pops hollered into the mouthpiece of the phone. "Well, can I book an appointment fer tomorrow ta see him? Yeah. What time? Just give me a minute," he turned to look at Eli and Jed. "Says tomorrow at one."

"*Ja, das gut,*" Eli smiled.

"Tomorrow at one is a good time," Pops hollered back into the mouthpiece. "See you then," and he clanged the receiver down on the cradle.

The next day, just before one o'clock, Pops chugged into town in a rusty relic of a car. Pops and the old Model-T were probably about the same age and temperament. His lawyer greeted him as soon as he entered the office. It was apparent the middle-aged, balding man knew Pops well.

"How're ya doin' Pops?"

"Good, real good. As a matter of fact, I couldn't be better! I'm finally goin' ta do it!" He said enthusiastically, "I'm goin' ta sell the farm while there's something left ta sell." Pops nodded, giving a broad smile that showed one too many spaces between his stained teeth.

"So, you're finally going to take the developer's offer?" The lawyer gave a broad toothy smile, rubbing his hands together with anticipation.

"That'll be the day!" Pop's smile disappeared. Eli and Jed entered the office at that moment, prompting the older man to make introductions. "They're going ta let me stay on at the farm, and they won't be dividin' it up to put up a subdivision either."

The lawyer scowled at Eli and Jed, obviously not approving of Pops's situation with these Amish men.

"Them developers wouldn't promise ta let me stay on fer a spell. I just don't think I could leave my Lottie. We had a lot of good memories in that old farmhouse," the old man's smile faded as he looked from Eli and Jed to the lawyer.

"Are you sure this is what you want to do?" The lawyer felt the deal of his life slipping through his fingers. "You wouldn't like to take a few days and think about it?" He tried to get more time to salvage his real estate shenanigans. "Maybe the developers can give you a better price."

"I couldn't be more sure of anything in my life, at least, right now," Pops assured the gaudily dressed attorney.

"Besides, getting' more money has nothin' ta do with it. These here men are willing to match the developer's price, an' that's good enough fer me," he turned back and nodded at Jed and Eli.

"Guess I don't have to tell you that you're buying a prime piece of real estate at a bargain price, gentleman," the lawyer looked from Jed to Eli, wondering how he could still benefit from this deal. "You have agreed to let Pops stay as long as he needs to?"

"*Ja, das* right," Eli nodded.

"Then, in Pop's best interests, I'm going to include that as one of the terms of the sale, and if you don't follow through, it will be a breach of contract," he threatened.

"*Ja, das gut,*" Eli nodded again, staring the lawyer, knowingly, in the eyes.

"Where exactly will Pops be living?" The man pressed on.

Eli stood a little straighter, towering over the stocky man. "There's an addition at the back of the *haus*, an' we're goin' ta put a bathroom in it an' fix it up. He's goin' ta continue livin' in the main part of the *haus* while we get it ready fer him."

"How much are you planning on charging him monthly to live there?"

"Nothing; it's one of the conditions of the sale." Eli looked levelly at the lawyer and thought. 'There's no way yer gettin' this farm.' He wondered if the lawyer was the developer trying to steal the farm for a song.

"Electrical?" The lawyer persisted.

"Not a thing; it'll be tied inta the main *haus*."

"Property taxes?" The lawyer continued to look for loopholes.

"I'll absorb this year. Any current outstanding can be taken out of the price of the farm." Eli stood tall and strong, refusing to back down to the lawyer's suspicious questions.

The lawyer tapped his pen on the leather-bound desk calendar, frowned, and finally looked at the older man. "That fair with you, Pops?" He asked, obviously disgruntled.

"The taxes are current," Pops informed them.

"Any other expenses you feel you might need to be compensated for?" The attorney tried again, looking Eli square in the eye.

"Nothing fer me," Eli assured him. "His own expenses might include the food he eats and his clothing." As if anticipating the lawyer's next barrage of questions, he added. "I'll pay fer a survey company ta *kumme* in an' make sure the property stakes are correct."

"Alright, I'll have my secretary type up the conditions of sale, then both parties can read it over to check for omissions and errors. I'll get you to sign off in the presence of myself and my secretary. Once your check has cleared the bank, you'll be the owner of one hundred acres of prime real estate."

"*Gut. Danke*," Eli smiled, turning to his dad. "Can ya think of anything else, *Dat*?"

"*Ja, das gut*," Jed smiled at him, pleased Eli had handled the transaction, and lawyer, so well.

One week later, the survey was completed, and the transaction with the lawyer was behind them. All the men employed at Yoder's Mill gathered bright and early at Eli's newly purchased farm. They replaced rotting roofing boards, hauled the heavy metal roofing up, and attached it to the wood on the roof of the enormous hip-roofed barn. The women brought lunch and set it out on makeshift tables. After lunch, the men got busy pitching out the musty rotting hay from the haymow and hauled it to an empty ravine at the back of the farm. Other men repaired the massive sliding door and remounted it on its track. They moved on to fix the swollen door in the lower part of the barn and dug back the silt and weeds that had collected over the years, preventing the door from operating correctly. By four o'clock, the men left for their respective homes, and the vast hip-roofed barn stood stately, given a new lease on life, ready to be set up for Eli's dairy operation.

Pops shook his head in disbelief and said to Tobiah, "Your men sure know how ta work."

"*Ja*, they're *gut* workers. Next week, we'll be here to start on the rooms at the back of the *haus*."

"Can't say I regret sellin' the old place ta young Eli.

You fellas will have it as good as new, maybe even better than when I had it in full swing."

Tobiah nodded and smiled, in complete agreement with Pops. "Eli will have this farm lookin' as *gut* as new, or my name ain't Tobiah Yoder."

When Esther came home on her weekend sabbatical, Eli was eager to show her the farm. "There's still more work ta be done, tons more work. But the barn has been restored an' *Onkle* an' his men insulated an' remodeled the back part of the *haus*. That way, Pops can live in it."

"Who's Pops?" Esther asked, excited at the prospect of seeing the farm.

"The *alt* man I bought the farm from. I gave him permission ta stay on the farm as long as he wants."

Esther smiled at him. "You've always been kind and generous, Eli. I'm glad I have you for my big *bruder*."

"Ya think I should be an *alt* crank?" He made a funny face at Esther.

Esther laughed, "You couldn't be, even if you tried."

Eli became serious, "I expect yer right. I could never live with myself if I suddenly became mean to others; it's just not who I am."

"So, when are we going?" Esther strove to regain the lighter, bantering mood between them.

"Let me check with *Dat* to see if'n he needs me this afternoon. Then I have a favor ta ask of ya?"

"*Ja*?" Esther smiled, knowing she could never deny Eli

anything. She might put on airs, but she knew she would do anything for Eli; he was just that kind of big brother.

"Do ya mind if'n we stop by an' pick Naomi up? We drove by the farm last weekend, but I know she can't wait ta look 'round inside." He looked sheepishly down at the ground.

Esther smiled kindly at Eli. "That's a *wunderbar* idea!" Then she jested lightly, "you can't expect her to live in it when you get married and not let her see it first."

He looked at her sharply, "but isn't that what Thomas is askin' ya ta do? Marry him, then go live somewhere ya never seen. Esther, that's more than a hundred miles away!"

Esther sobered. "I haven't promised myself to him."

"That's not how he's been talkin' 'round." Eli immediately clammed up but thought. 'I even saw him drivin' Mary-Lou home the other night.' He was barely able to hold his own counsel.

Esther sighed, "*Bruder*, that's why you mean the whole world to me. You care. But I'll tell you right now; if he doesn't believe in Bible truths like we do, he can wait until the *couws kumme* home because I'm not going against *Gott's* word."

"*Be ye not unevenly yoked. ~ 2 Corinthians 6:14.*" Eli agreed and gave Esther a quick hug.

"What's that for?" Esther laughed and yet, at the same time, looked suitably surprised.

"Cause ya was always my best student," he smiled broadly.

"Well, I'm not sure if that's a compliment or not since I've been your only one," Esther frowned in mock bewilderment.

They both laughed. Their brother and sister bonding had begun the day Jed carried Esther into their home and family and would last for the rest of their lives. Often, they would look back on these moments in time with fond memories.

Esther challenged, "You better get your work done, or we aren't going anywhere. I think *Dat* needs you. He's standing in the doorway with his arms crossed."

They both turned to face their dad, and Eli sprinted toward the barn, while Esther raised her hand in acknowledgment before turning toward the house.

"What was that all about?" Jed scowled at his son.

"What's that, *Dat*?"

"Laughin' then given yer *schwester* a hug."

Eli took a moment and told Jed of the exchange, including his suspicions of Thomas two-timing Esther with Mary-Lou, then shared Esther's response.

"Fer sure?" Jed's face held a note of relief.

"As our heavenly *Vater* is my witness," Eli nodded, satisfied he could deliver some good news to his parent.

Jed gave him a quick hug, "Ya just lifted a ton weight off my shoulders, *sohn*."

"It would seem hugs are the order of the day," Eli

grinned at his dad. 'I wonder who the third will be?' Eli thought, recalling that most things came in threes. Before he forgot, he turned to his dad, "I got a favor ta ask."

"What's that?" Jed sobered.

"I was goin' ta take the girls ta see the farm. Can ya do without me fer a while after lunch?"

Jed's face lit up, "Are ya goin' ta pick Naomi up so she can have a look see?"

"*Ja*, if'n ya don't need the family buggy," Eli looked toward his dad but couldn't quite meet his eyes.

"Don't suppose ya want any taggers-along?" Jed asked hopefully.

Eli looked at the barn floor, then up at his dad, "Maybe not this time, *Dat*. I don't want Naomi feelin' we're swoopin' down on her."

"*Ja*, I expect yer right," Jed agreed. "Let's get these stalls done. Then we can wash the barn smells off of us before lunch."

"*Ja, Danke Dat*." Eli proceeded to muck out the stalls with his usual gusto.

~ ~ ~

The way of a fool is right in his own eyes,
But a wise man is he who listens to counsel
~ Proverbs 12:15 ~

CHAPTER 12
Perusing the New Home

Eli and Esther were on the road at one o'clock, leaving the family farm in their parent's family buggy. Eva and Jed waved them off while standing in the middle of the drive. Jed glanced down at Eva and wondered at her confused expression.

"Now, why wouldn't he have taken his buggy?" She pondered, mystified.

"Cause, I expect he figured three would be a little crowded in his two-seater."

"Three? You don't suppose they might be picking Naomi up, do you?" Eva's face transformed into a beaming, hopeful grin.

"There's no supposin' about it. That's where Eli's headed right now," Jed chuckled at Eva's elated look. "I got somethin' else ta tell ya," he confided.

Eva looked at him expectantly, the pleased grin still plastered on her face.

"*Kumme*, let's sit awhile." He took hold of her hand and led her to the swing seat on the porch. There he told Eva of Eli's earlier exchange with Esther.

"You're sure about this? You're not just saying that, so I'll stop worrying about Esther?" Eva pressed.

"I'm tellin' ya exactly what Eli said when I asked him the same question. As our heavenly *Vater* is my witness."

Eva hugged Jed, then quickly composed herself folding her hands on her lap. Regardless, she couldn't control her elated spirits.

Jed chuckled, smiling at her, and placed his arm around her shoulder. "We're not too *alt* fer a hug, are we?" He teased gently as Eva crimsoned. "And still not to *alt* ta be my blushin' bride. Ain't so?" He chuckled.

Eli and Esther drove one and a half concessions to the Woerner farm. Esther was pleased Eli was including Naomi on their trip for a closer look at the farm he'd just purchased. She understood that Naomi's opinion would hold more value to Eli than anyone else.

Naomi's mother stood in front of the kitchen window washing the baking dishes at the sink when she spied the Kuepfer buggy coming in the drive. "Eli's *kumming,* and he's got their family buggy."

Naomi stopped paring apples and stood on her toes to look over her mother's shoulder. "Do you think I should go out and greet him?"

"*Nee*, your *Daed's kummin'* outa the barn. He can find out what's going on."

"*Ach, Mamma,* Esther's with him!" Naomi exclaimed excitedly, anticipating visiting with her old friend.

"*Ja*, I heard she and Hannah went on *rumspringa* together. They're probably home for the weekend." Secretly she wished Charles would have let Naomi go too, but he had strictly forbidden it.

"Your *Daed's* nodding his head and *kumming* toward the *haus*. Go back to what you were doing and let him have his say." They turned back to the table and began rolling out pastry and blending the sliced apples with sugar and cinnamon, adding a squeeze of lemon.

Boots stomping on the porch announced his arrival, but he opened the door rather than remove his boots. "Can ya do without Naomi fer a while? Eli and Esther Kuepfer have *kumme* callin' an' want ta take her out fer a short time."

Anna looked at her husband, not wanting to appear overly interested for fear he would change his mind. "*Ja*, we're done here."

He nodded his head once and closed the door.

Naomi and her mother smiled at one another. "*Schnell*!" Anna pushed. "Pull your choring apron off and put this clean one on. Get your hair tucked under your Prayer *kappe*. If your *Daed* doesn't think you're presentable, he may not let you go, especially in broad daylight. And sit in the back with Esther." Seeing her daughter standing in the middle of the kitchen, frozen, Anna shooed Naomi. "*Schnell*! He's waiting to see you off."

"Do I look neat?" Naomi stood before her mother for

inspection.

"*Ja*. Now go! Don't run; walk quietly. Here's your bonnet," she handed Naomi her head covering.

Naomi knew exactly what her mother meant. There was no sense in upsetting her dad for some little thing done wrong. She tucked some wayward strands of flaxen hair under her Prayer *kappe*, lowered her bonnet, and walked off the porch as demurely as possible. Taking her mom's advice, she climbed into the buggy and took her place beside Esther.

Eli looked over his shoulder to ensure they were settled and turned the horse in the yard. "We'll be back this side of two hours," he nodded to Naomi's dad.

"I know ya will," the older man returned the nod. From experience, he knew Eli was a young man of his word. On top of that, to add to his credibility, Eli had just bought a farm. "*Mann* after my own thinkin'," Charles Woerner muttered, smiling. He was pleased with himself for having raised such a fine daughter that Naomi was worthy of attracting a man like Eli. Satisfied with his day, he strode to the house, kicked his boots off, and sat at the kitchen table to watch his wife put the finishing touches on the pies before putting them in the oven.

"Have ya got enough wood?" He asked.

Anna peered in the wood box kept near the wood-burning stove. "*Ja*, there's lots here." Wondering why her husband was lingering in the house, she asked, "Do you want some *kaffee*?"

"*Ja, das gut*," he agreed. He cleared his throat while she poured coffee into a cup and added a dash of cream and two teaspoons of sugar - just the way he liked it. "I just wanted to tell ya, Eli Kuepfer has just bought himself a farm."

Anna's heart skipped a beat, but she answered levelly. "*Ach*, that's *gut* to hear."

"So, I was thinkin' he'll be lookin' fer a *frau*."

She looked over at him, and her mouth dropped open in complete shock.

He ignored her and went on. "Knowin' how close ya are ta the girl, I don't want ya ta say nothin' against it. She won't find anyone any better, anywhere. An' I can't look after her forever. Better ta marry her off now, then fer her ta be an *alt maidel*." 'There, I said it,' he stared absently into his coffee cup with an inward sigh.

Anna suppressed her elation. "Whatever you think is best for our *tochter*, Charles."

"*Ja*. Well, that's it." He stood slowly as one with a heavy burden on his shoulders. Then added as if clearing his conscience, "Naomi is the youngest of our five *kinder*. Two got lost ta *rumspringa*, and the other two married without my permission. That leaves Naomi." He worked his jaw, finally admitting, "I have no intention of doin' wrong by our one remainin' *kinder*. I'll see her married inta a *gut* family. One outa five ain't a *gut* average, but she'll be twenty soon – almost an *alt maidel*." Charles shrugged and left the kitchen, unaware of the tears in Anna's eyes at his words.

Eli, Esther, and Naomi chatted above, around, and at each other. "Where are we going?" Naomi asked, intrigued they would ask her to go with them and more astounded that her dad had agreed.

"To see Eli's farm, silly goose," Esther replied, smiling at her friend.

"Did you tell my *Daed* that?" She asked, surprised.

"*Ja*," Eli turned in the seat and smiled at her. "He's not so bad," he defended Charles Woerner. "He's just from the *alt* school. I just tell him what I'm goin' ta do an' keep my promise. Any *mann* wants that fer his family." By this time, they were turning into the drive of Eli's farm, flanked on both sides with weeds and shrubs that had gone wild.

"I'll tie the horse an' go ask Pops if'n we can look 'round."

"Pops?" both girls chimed together.

"*Ja*. His real name is Neil Edwards, but he likes ta be called Pops."

While Esther and Naomi climbed out of the buggy, Eli tied the horse to a tree. They didn't have to look for the older man; he came out of the house with a broad smile.

"There's the young man," he pumped Eli's hand up and down numerous times and looked at the girls.

"This is my *schwester*, Esther, and our friend, Naomi." Eli made the introductions.

Pops nodded at the girls, then excitedly turned back to Eli. "Have I got a surprise for you. Come and see what they did with the back part of the house," Pops led the way in his hobbling gait.

Esther and Naomi glanced at the house's main part, horrified by how the older man was living. As if sensing their thoughts, Pops apologized, "sorry fer the mess. Since my Lottie's gone, I just don't have any interest in keepin' things up."

"Don't worry, Pops. We'll clean it up, and it'll be like a new *haus*," Eli reassured him.

"If you do it as nice as the part ya did fer me, it'll be real nice. But come on back." He led them down the hall to the rooms at the back of the house, opened the door, and stood back to proudly display the newly renovated rooms. It was almost as if he had done the renovations himself.

"*Ach,* this is nice," Esther smiled.

"And bright," Naomi agreed.

"There's one problem," Pops raised his bushy eyebrows and shook his head. "There's no way I'll get everything in here."

Eli looked at him, then at Esther and Naomi, stumped.

In her soft voice, Naomi suggested, "There's lots of room for some of your favorite furniture in here, and important paperwork can be stored in totes and put in a safe place somewhere."

"That's a good idea," Pops agreed and turned to Eli. "When do ya think I should move in?"

"Let's give it another week to let the smell of the paint settle, then my *Daed* and I will *kumme* an' help ya move."

"You'd do that for me?" The old-timer smiled at Eli.

"Fer sure an' fer certain. We're like family, ain't so?"

"I guess we are kinda. My daughter lives out in Denver, over in Colorado, and she's too busy with her career ta come ta visit."

"Then not to worry. We can be yer adopted family." Eli looked at Esther and smiled, thinking of the success of their own adoptions.

"If you want to look through the rest of the house, go ahead," Pops offered. "Just remember, I never claimed to be a housekeeper, and I don't plan on being one in my old age, either."

"We understand," Eli responded kindly.

"Well, go ahead," Pops encouraged. "I never use the upstairs; it's too hard on my knees to climb them anymore. I haven't been up there since Lottie's been gone." He sat down in a threadbare rocker recliner and put it into motion.

"Just a quick tour," Eli reminded them. "I don't want to be late getting Naomi home."

They stepped lightly up a stately staircase covered with well-worn runners. The handrail was made of oak; the hand-turned spindles added to its air of grandeur. Naomi ran her hand appreciatively up the railing as they climbed the steps. "This looks so grand," she smiled up at Esther and Eli, then hurried to catch up with them.

There were three bedrooms and a bathroom upstairs. Everything was coated with layers of dust, and old dead houseflies carpeted the hardwood floors.

"It needs a *gut* airing," Esther sneezed.

"Let's go back downstairs." Eli took a quick inventory. "At least we know what's up here. There are no leaks in the roof, and the pipes in the bathroom look *gut*."

Esther and Naomi took another quick look in each room, longing to explore more. In one of the back bedrooms, they spied a set of steps that led upward; a trap door was at the top of the steps, presumably leading up to the attic. They squeezed each other's hands excitedly, knowing further exploring would have to wait for another time. Eli was right; it was important to keep his promise to Naomi's dad and be back in plenty of time.

Back downstairs, they did a quick look-through. Pops had fallen asleep in his chair and was snoring lightly. There was a large kitchen-sitting area, a two-piece bath, and a room Pops used as his bedroom. However, judging by the rows of shelving around the walls, it was probably a library at one time. A small area next to the kitchen would make a good pantry and mud room, and a door led to the outside. Naomi noticed an old, rusting, chipped enamel wringer washer in the mudroom.

"Let's go out this door," Eli opened the door, and they stood on a spacious back porch with a distinctive tilt. "This will need to be replaced," Eli murmured. A pulley clothesline stretched from the house out over the backyard, strung higher at the furthest reach so any wet clothes hanging on it would catch a cross breeze and dry quicker. "Anything else you want to look at?" He asked.

"Is there lots of room in the basement?" Naomi asked.

"*Ja*. There's lots of room, but it needs some work. There's lots of shelves for canning. I even saw some boxes with sealer jars in them," knowing that piece of information would please any Amish woman.

"Really?" Naomi smiled excitedly.

"*Ja*, ready fer someone ta move in and make it a home again," Eli took her hand and held it as he looked into her eyes.

"Let's see the barn really quick before we have to leave," Esther interrupted the couple's moment, taking a long step off the wooden deck to avoid using the dilapidated steps. Her words nudged Eli and Naomi into completing the tour before it was time to go.

"It's a huge barn," Naomi ogled at the spaciousness of the loft.

"*Ja*, an' I'll need every bit of it to set up my *milchin'* operation. There's still a lot of work, but all in *gut* time. What do ya think about white washin' everythin'?"

"Wooden fencing, too?" Naomi looked at him optimistically.

"Fencin' too," he agreed and smiled at her. 'She's the sweetest girl I ever met. Always asking, never assuming.'

They got Naomi home with ample time to spare, and as expected, her dad had been waiting for their arrival. He came out of the barn and headed the horse, looking at Naomi. "I expect yer *Mamm* is waitin' on yer help."

"*Ja, Dat.*" Naomi turned to thank Esther and Eli for including her, then disappeared into the house.

"How'd it go?" Charles Woerner looked directly at Eli.

"*Gut*, real *gut*. I'd like ta take ya over some time. Maybe ya could give me some ideas on settin' up fer a *milchin'* operation since ya have such a *gut* operation here." Eli looked about the well-groomed fields, contented cattle, and well-fed draft horses.

"*Ja*, I'd be right pleased, but runnin' a dairy operation is a lot of work."

Eli nodded respectfully. "Work never bothered me. How'd it be if'n I stop by Wednesday afternoon and pick you up? Just past lunch?"

"*Ja, das gut.* Why don't ya *kumme* fer lunch, then we can get on our way, straight afterward."

"*Ja.*" Eli nodded slowly in contemplation. "*Das gut.* I'll see ya Wednesday at lunchtime, round noon, then."

"Round noon," Charles nodded in agreement and watched Eli turn the horse and head out the drive.

Naomi and her mother busied themselves in the kitchen when they saw Charles Woerner head toward the house. His heavy work boots clunked as they hit the floor just before he came inside.

"Make somethin' nice fer lunch *kumme* Wednesday. Eli is *kummin'* over, an' we're goin' ta have a look at the place he just bought. He wants my help in settin' up fer dairy farmin'," Charles Woerner nodded his head; a smile of importance and self-satisfaction lit his face.

Anna smiled at him. It was the first time she'd seen him look this happy in a long time, and it warmed her heart to see the old him – the way he used to be before their children had all left to do their own thing. As surely as she stood in their big roomy kitchen, she knew that was why he'd changed. He was strict, but he was also a product of an overbearing parent himself.

"Naomi, *kumme* sit with yer *alt Daed*." Charles requested.

Naomi readily obeyed; she wouldn't have done anything but and sat on a chair across the table from him.

He placed his large hands on the table, interlocked his fingers, looked at them as if contemplating his words, and cleared his throat. "I'll tell ya exactly what I told yer *Mamm*. If'n that young *mann* asks ya ta marry him, yer ta accept."

Naomi crimsoned and nodded her head.

"An' don't be in a hurry ta grow up an' go gettin' inta things ya have no right gettin' inta until after yer married." He cleared his throat again.

Naomi didn't know what he was talking about, but she nodded anyway.

"Ya need ta keep yerself fer yer *mann*, if'n ya know what I mean."

Anna gasped, and Naomi blanched, then blushed again, mortified.

"Well, it's only right," his voice rose defensively.

"*Ja, Dat*," Naomi squeaked.

"Ya best get helpin' yer *Mamm* with supper," he instructed gruffly, then pushed the chair back and stood up.

Anna wrapped a warm turnover in a piece of paper and placed it in his hand. "Something to hold you over 'til supper."

Charles stopped and looked into her eyes. "*Danke*," he muttered and continued to stand before her. She knew he was trying to put something into words, but because he was a man who had not been allowed to express himself as a child, he often didn't know how to. It would become bottled up inside of him, spilling out often negatively. "She's the only one we got left. I just want ta do right by her an' help her the best we can."

Anna smiled into his eyes, "we're doing the best we know how. Eli Kuepfer is such a nice young *mann*."

"*Ja*, an' he's honorable, an' I like that." He left the kitchen and headed toward the barn, munching on the flakey turnover as he went.

Anna hugged her daughter, "What will we have for lunch on Wednesday?"

Instead of answering, Naomi looked at her mother, eyes

huge, filled with horror. She squeaked with a gulp, "I'm just glad Eli didn't hear what he said, or I'd never be able to face him again."

Her mother sighed, "*Ja*, sometimes your *Daed* hasn't the best way of expressing himself, but he means well, and he really does care about you. Ever since your *bruders* and *schwester* left, he's so afraid of losing you too."

"It's not hard to see why they left," Naomi shook her head, appalled.

"Stay strong, *tochter*, and *Gott* will reward you greatly. Now tell me about this farm Eli bought."

As Esther and Eli went out the drive of the Woerner farm, Esther murmured, "I'd sure hate to be on his wrong side."

"*Ach*, he's not so bad. How'd ya think ya'd feel if'n four of yer *kinder* just up an' left. He's just protectin' Naomi from freeloaders." He didn't say but wanted to add, 'like Thomas.'

"*Ja*. I guess you're right. But I'm glad *Dat* isn't like that."

~ ~ ~

Children, obey your parents in everything,
for this pleases the Lord
~ Colossians 3:20 ~

CHAPTER 13
Home for Supper

Eli and Esther chatted about the changes that Eli wanted to make on the farm he'd purchased. As they approached the Kuepfer drive, they were surprised to see Thomas coming down the road toward them. They were even more surprised when he followed them up the drive. Pulling up beside them, he didn't bother getting out of his buggy but leaned his elbows on his knees and addressed Eli. "I heard ya bought a farm," he smiled stiffly at Eli.

"My *Daed* an' I did, but he'll continue ta manage this farm, an' I'll manage the other one." Eli returned his look levelly, knowing where Thomas was headed.

"Do ya think ya might need help?"

"I'll let ya know if'n I *kumme* up short. Right know *Onkle* an' his men are about all I can handle financially," he laughed, but Esther could tell it was a forced laugh.

Jed came out of the barn, held Eli's horse, and nodded to their visitor. "How are ya, Thomas?"

"*Gut,*" Thomas returned the nod.

"Are ya stayin' fer supper?" Jed asked.

Esther was shocked at her dad's invitation, and by the look on his face, so was Thomas. "*Ja, das gut,*" he accepted, nodding.

"*Gut,* then *kumme* ta the barn and help with chores while Esther tells her *Mamm* we have company stayin'."

Eli looked skeptically at his dad. 'He's got somethin' up his sleeve, if'n I know *Daed.*'

"Ya can take yer horse outa the shafts an' put him in that field," Jed offered.

"Naw, I'll tie him ta that tree," Thomas refused the offer.

"Then yer *willkommen* ta give him some hay," Jed persisted.

"Naw, it's alright."

"Water?"

"Naw."

Esther looked round-eyed from the horse to Thomas and then at her dad.

Jed raised an eyebrow at her while Eli stood with his arms crossed, feet planted apart – not a typical Amish stance, especially not one for Eli.

"Thomas, what is your horse's name?" She looked at the animal's damp shoulder, sticky from sweating after a long drive.

"Name? Horse, I guess," he laughed, dismissing her while leading the horse over to a tree.

Esther's dad's half-closed eyes followed him as he chewed on the inside of his mouth.

"He didn't even say *hallo* to me," Esther murmured to Eli. "Do you suppose he's forgotten my name?"

"I doubt it. It's just his way," Eli returned with a grimace.

"But you always talk to Naomi and call her by name."

"We're two different kinds of men," Eli returned.

"And *Daed* does too," she persisted, searching for some logic to Thomas' behavior.

"Again, they're as different as day an' night," Eli raised his eyebrows at her.

Esther frowned and sat looking at Eli, not saying anything.

"Esther, do ya want ta get outa the buggy so's I can put the horse an' buggy away?" Eli snapped testily. Nothing annoyed him more than a man that wouldn't look after his animal. 'It's a short hop to lookin' after a family,' he thought, perturbed, unwrapping the holdback strap from the buggy shafts.

"*Ach. Ja,*" Esther acknowledged Eli's request, climbed down quickly, and went up to the house, deep in thought.

"Esther, wait a minute," Jed called after her before turning and speaking to Eli. "I'll be down in a minute. *Dawdi* is feedin' the calves. Why don't ya go ahead an' have Thomas help tie the *couws* in the *milchin'* stanchions."

The two groups separated, and Esther walked beside her dad toward the house. When they got to where the horse was tied to the tree, Jed turned and watched Eli and Thomas until they disappeared into the barn. "I'd like ta tie him ta a tree without food or water. It wouldn't hurt ta give the horse some water. At least he took the horse outa the shafts an' pushed the buggy back," he mumbled, disgruntled.

"I have an idea, *Dat*." Esther looked at her parent with a sparkle in her eyes.

Jed looked at her suspiciously.

"I wonder how *gut* he tied the horse to this tree. The horse might just get loose and start eating the grass in the yard."

"Ya mean with a little help?" Jed chuckled with a wink. "Let me give it a drink." He quickly fetched a pail of water out of the water trough.

"I shut the gate in case he gets loose. That way, he'll stay in the yard." Esther met her dad back at the horse.

Jed chuckled, glad he had such a quick-thinking daughter. "*Ja, das* a *gut* idea."

They went their separate ways again, Esther to the house and Jed to the barn. Every so often, Esther would look out the kitchen window.

"Why do you keep looking out that window?" May finally asked.

"I'm just making sure the horse is still tied," Esther answered nonchalantly.

"You could always close the gate, and if it gets loose, it'll stay in the yard," Eva suggested.

"It is," Esther smiled mischievously at her mom.

"I'm not sure why, but this whole thing has your *Daed* written all over it," Eva looked closely at Esther.

"*Dat* and me!" Esther smiled cheekily.

"The apple don't fall far from the tree," May murmured, but laughter was in her eyes. She looked out the window at the tied horse; they all took turns keeping an eye on the poor animal. Fifteen minutes later, May joyfully announced, "The horse is loose! And he's eating grass."

"*Gut*," Eva responded. "That grass was getting long anyway. It'll save Eli cutting it." She returned to work on the meal for supper, not concerned one iota.

Eli emerged from the barn first, saw the loose horse eating the grass in the yard, and chuckled. "I need ta put yer horse on my payroll, Thomas. Now I don't have as much grass ta cut." He picked up the dragging leash still attached to the halter. "*Danke, alt* fella," he patted the horse on the neck and tied him to the tree, leaving lots of slack in the line.

Thomas squinted his eyes in contemplation as he looked at the horse.

"Let's see what the womenfolk have fer supper?" Gideon passed them all and headed for the house.

The men washed up at the outside hand pump. They stomped onto the porch and removed their boots before filing into the kitchen.

"Go ahead and sit down," Eva directed. "And we'll bring the food over."

Thomas sat next to Eli, which placed him across from Esther. After silent prayer and following Jed's "Amen," everyone began passing the food toward Gideon, except Thomas. As the eldest man at the table, he was always served first, but Thomas, ignoring table etiquette, helped himself before passing the food dishes to Gideon. Gideon sat up straighter in his chair and gruffly, "Harrumphed." Jed knew the look from experience and cleared his throat.

"*Danke* fer yer help with chores, Thomas," he prompted, making an excuse for small talk.

"*Ja*," Thomas nodded and kept eating.

"Does our farm remind ya of yer home in Lucknow?" Jed continued.

"Naw, this is a lot more work." Thomas kept his eyes on the food before him as he continued shoveling.

Jed gave up trying to draw him into a conversation, sharing an exasperated look with Eva.

"I hope we don't talk too much, but it's the only time we can share what happened each day," Eva half apologized.

Thomas shrugged his shoulders without looking at her. "*Das gut*. Back home, we don't talk durin' meals. *Daed* says ya swallow too much air when ya talk an' eat; it makes the stomach *krank*."

"Interestin'," Gideon sat back and grimaced.

Jed shook his head slightly at his dad.

Gideon smiled wryly. "Got mostly beef cattle then, have ya?"

"Mostly."

"It must be a lot of work feedin' beef cattle ta make them ready fer *markt*?" Gideon persisted.

"Naw, we just leave them on pasture all summer, sell the calves in the fall an' feed hay ta the *couws* in the winter."

"No grain or silage?" Gideon asked, flabbergasted.

"Naw costs too much. *Daed* says it takes away from the overhead."

"Next time we get a tough rump roast from The *Markt*, I'll know where it came from." That ended the conversation before he remembered his stomach. "What're we havin' fer dessert?" He looked at May.

"The day he don't ask fer dessert, I'll know he's sick," May chuckled.

Thomas sat back and belched.

Esther glanced at him, horrified. 'That's disgusting! Who belches at the table?' Then she remembered herself and gave him the benefit of the doubt. 'Well, maybe it's acceptable where he kummes from.'

Thomas followed the men to the porch without acknowledging or showing gratitude to the women. Drinking his coffee, he looked at Jed, "If'n ya ever need help, let me know since I'll be stayin' in the area fer awhile."

"*Ja*, we can always use help durin' harvestin'. An'

we'll be needin' help ta move Eli's *milch couws* once we get that operation up an' runnin'. Yer lookin' fer work, are ya?"

"*Ja.*"

"What do ya know best?"

"Beef."

"I see." Jed nodded and thought, 'an' by what ya said at the supper table, ya don't.' "Tobiah Yoder, across the way, is always lookin' fer help. Are ya any *gut* with a hammer?"

"Not really."

Jed cringed inwardly and chose to ignore Thomas' answer. "Tamorrow, stop by an' see him; he might can use ya ta stack lumber."

Thomas shrugged and stood up. "I'll look in on it. *Danke* fer supper." He stepped off the porch, put his horse into the buggy, and drove off without so much as a nod.

Agitated, Eli stood up. "Ya can't let Esther marry him, *Dat*! He'd never fit in with this family. It's a *gut* job she went on *rumspringa*, ain't?"

"Why do ya think I had him stay on fer supper? So, she could see fer herself." Jed shook his head in disbelief.

"He's not much at workin' in the barn either," Gideon grunted, adding his displeasure.

"I'd say he never had a *gut* teacher," Jed concluded. "It's a shame, a real shame, that a young *mann* like him has no future."

~ ~ ~

*...For we will all stand before the judgement seat of God.
Each one of us will give an account of himself to God
~ Romans 14: 10,12 ~*

CHAPTER 14
Home Cookin'

Eli arrived at the Woerner's for lunch just before noon. He took the horse from between the shafts, tied him to a tree, and hung a net filled with hay for the animal to munch on.

Charles Woerner came out of the barn. "*Gut* timin'," he smiled, and they walked to the house together. Following silent prayer, the men talked of farming and milk quotas until it was time to leave.

"*Danke* fer lunch," Eli smiled at Anna and Naomi. "It's a *gut* job I'm not goin' ta be diggin' post holes after that *gut* meal. I don't think I could." He chuckled, rubbed his stomach, followed his host to the porch, and pulled his boots on.

"Ya have a nice farm," Eli commented as they drove leisurely by some of Charles' well-tended fields. "What ya plannin' on doin' with it when ya retire?"

Charles shrugged, "My *älteste* was supposed ta take it over. Now, I don't know."

"What's he doin' now?" Eli asked.

"Last I heard, managin' a *milchin'* operation in Oxford County."

"So, he stayed in farmin'?" Eli nodded.

"*Ja*," the older man nodded his head without enlarging.

"If'n he's anythin' like you, he runs a *gut* operation," Eli complimented.

"He should. He learned the right way," Charles returned with a huff.

"Is there any chance we could have a look-see that operation?"

Something akin to a shadow passed across Charles' face.

"I was thinkin' it'd be a *gut* idea ta inspect other operations before buildin' mine." Eli pressed and clucked to his horse to get it trotting. He continued. "Ta see what works an' what don't. It only makes sense ta me before puttin' a lot of money out before buildin' mine. *Ja*?"

"Let's see what space ya have, then inspect mine." Charles' jaw tightened. "One day we could go fer a drive, but it'd be an all-day trip,"

"*Ja, das gut*, real *gut*," Eli smiled at his friend.

Eli was surprised to see the usually stoic Charles become animated as they conducted a thorough inspection of the empty barn.

"I'm thinkin' ya might want ta pull out the pens an' build new ones fer calves. Leave three or four standin' stalls fer horses, an' a *gut* size foalin' box. Ya need somewhere ta keep the *milch* cool 'til the tanker picks it up. Ya can always build a *milch haus*, at the front of the barn ta wash yer equipment when yer finished with the *milchin'*. Along that wall," he pointed out. "Would be a *gut* place fer the *milch* platform. Ya should get ten *milchin'* stalls in there, easy."

Eli nodded his head, storing the information Charles was giving him.

"It's goin' ta cost ya a lot ta set up. More than what it cost me when I set up fer my operation," Charles forewarned.

"*Ja*, I expect it will, but then I plan on hangin' around a while. An' this *alt* barn ain't goin' nowhere either," Eli looked around the huge area, pleased.

"*Ja*, it's a *gut,* solid barn. Ya did *gut* gettin' it. Are ya still wantin' ta go ta that *milchin'* operation in Oxford?" Charles drew himself up and looked at Eli.

"*Ja*. If'n ya can find the time ta go with me. I have no idea where it is," Eli returned.

"It might be a *gut* thing ta go an' see if'n my boy is any *gut* at managin' a dairy farm," Charles remarked thoughtfully

"It'll be *gut* ta see him again." Eli raised his eyebrows and looked over at the older man.

"Then, how be we plan on goin' next week? We could leave right after chores in the mornin' so we can be back in time fer the evenin' chores."

"*Ja*," Eli nodded his head, thinking. "It could work. I'll check with *Dat* if'n he can do chores fer me." He nodded again, looking at Charles. "I'm lookin' forward ta goin'," Eli smiled, pleased with how their day had turned out.

~.~.~.~

Sunday, following the Meeting, Esther and Hannah caught a northbound bus headed back to Julia's. Both girls were laden with home-baked goodies, the warm smells filling the bus's interior. When they finally arrived at their home away from home, their treasures overwhelmed Julia's refrigerator.

"I don't know about you," Esther enlightened her friend once they had settled back into their room. "But I have a ton of homework to do for classes this week."

"Me too. Is there anything we can study together since most of our classes are the same?"

"That essay, the professor, assigned on Money Management, has me stumped." Esther's eyebrows knitted together in contemplation.

"That's not so hard. First is the offering we give each Meeting. Then *kummes* business expenses, housing, transportation, food, and emergencies. That's how I'd do it anyway," Hannah remarked.

"*Ja*. That's what usually comes to mind. But I can't help thinking the Professor is looking for something else. I'm not sure he's looking for us to submit a budget; I think it is more along the line of different ways we can manage money." Esther looked across the room, deep in thought, while Hannah began to see the difference.

161

"Then there's our evening adult class in typing at the high school. How does one practice typing without a computer or a typewriter?" Hannah complained.

Esther looked at her as if a light had come on, "*Danke*, Hannah!"

"For what? Complaining?"

Both girls laughed.

Esther declared, "I'm going to ask *Daed* if I can use some of my college money to buy a second-hand typewriter. That way, we can practice here. Otherwise, we'll always need to go to the computer lab at school to practice our typing skills. We're ages behind the rest as it is." She continued thinking out loud. "Now, all I have to do is convince the Professor in this essay. But I'm not sure he'll think buying a typewriter is worthwhile." Esther went into deep thought mode and began thinking about her essay. Grabbing a pad of paper, she began writing furiously. 'Now, where will I find a typewriter to type this essay. I really can't hand in a handwritten essay, especially not when I want the Professor to think a typewriter is a *gut* investment.' Esther got a faraway look in her eyes. 'This is a 'pre-typewriter' essay meant to be convincing.' A smile crossed her face, and she jotted down more words for her project outline.

"Don't forget," Hannah reminded. "We need to study for end-of-semester exams."

Esther looked up from writing; her mouth dropped in shocked realization. "*Ja*. I near forgot. They are *kumming* up soon, aren't they?"

"Do you want me to set up times for studying together? That way, we can fit in a couple of courses a week before exams," Hannah looked at Esther questioningly.

"*Ja*. That would be a *gut* idea. And, if we are missing any important information, we'll still have time to talk with our professors."

"I'll make up a new schedule." Hannah pulled out a blank piece of paper and began an outline. "After I'm done, can you check it over to see if it conflicts with anything you're doing?"

"I can only think of going home every two weeks." Esther returned without looking up from her writing.

The two girls followed the new schedule, thankful toward the end of their studies to have it. Before the exams, it was as if they were on autopilot. Every morning, religiously, they consulted Hannah's schedule. Sometimes, they needed to check it more than once during the day to keep focused. So, when exams came, all one and a half weeks of them, the guideline helped see them through an already difficult time. They were exhausted, but their training at home to remain focused on the job at hand carried them through.

At the end of the grueling tests, Julia had planned a surprise for them. Remembering how the girls had devoured her spaghetti and meatballs whenever she had made it, she had a treat in store for them. Looking at their tired faces and the dark bags under their eyes, she decided to end the test week by celebrating. So, with the week of testing finally behind them, the girls met Julia at the Café Bus Stop downtown.

Julia led them across the street to an alleyway. The girls looked about as they walked down the dark alley, more terrified than mystified.

"Where are you taking us?" Hannah whispered, afraid to talk out loud. In her mind, only robbers would frequent a dark alley like this one.

"Just a little further," Julia encouraged.

A cat scurried from behind a garbage drum and ran ahead of them, frantically looking for a place to hide. The cat scared Esther and Hannah half to death. It wasn't an encouraging sign.

When Julia led them down cement steps to a basement entrance, both girls were really having second and third thoughts. The only lighting was an industrial-style shade with an oversized light bulb shining over the door, showing them a sign. It was a small Italian restaurant. Getting there had been a new experience for the girls.

The door opened inward, revealing a quaint, albeit dark, restaurant. Booths, made of rustic wood, lined the walls, absorbing the sound and lighting.

Their waiter handed them menus and took their drink order. Leaning across the table, Julia helped Esther and Hannah understand the menu since each dish was named in Italian. Fortunately, an English description was included on the menu. Thinking she was being safe, Esther chose spaghetti and meatballs. Being a little more adventurous,

Hannah selected a dish she couldn't pronounce the name of, Bucatini.

While waiting for their dishes to arrive, the three women took in their surroundings. Esther looked at the adjoining booth, thinking how delicious the other patron's food looked. Before long, a couple of waiters arrived with their dinner. Their eyes rounded at the oversized portions before them, but it was the most delicious spaghetti and meatballs Esther had ever eaten. They all chuckled. Hannah thought she was being adventurous, but it turned out that her pasta was a thick spaghetti-like noodle with a hole running through its center.

When they left the little restaurant, Esther remarked. "I'll never look at a dark alley the same way again!"

Both girls led the way to the bus stop, prepared to go home.

"Come on! We're not finished yet." Julia called them back to follow her.

Esther and Hannah looked at each other, shrugged, and hurried to catch up with their friend.

They stopped at a small wooden shelter. Minutes later, an old-fashioned street trolley, pulled by a team of white draft horses, stopped on the street before them. Following Julia, they boarded and asked excitedly. "Where are we going?"

"You'll have to wait and see," Julia settled back on the bench, a wide mysterious grin. No matter how the girls badgered her, she didn't give in.

"*Ach*. Look!" Esther pointed, captivated by all the lighted trees in Victoria Park. As if on cue, snow began falling. It drifted down, settling on the frozen ground and swirling lazily around the old Victorian street lamps. They stared in awe, pale cheeks turning red in the cold evening air; they were entering a true winter wonderland. Julia pointed out the different paths they could venture down and explore and the lit-up trees surrounding an ice rink. They walked down some of the paths in the park, looking at the lights, "Oohing and awing." People called out Christmas greetings and pointed to a nearby stand. "A vendor is selling hot chocolate and homemade cookies!"

They returned the Christmas greetings and headed toward the amphitheater with an ice rink in front of it. It was a fantastic way to begin their Christmas break, away from the rigors of exams. Back at their friend's home, they thanked Julia profusely. It was an exciting way to begin their Christmas and an evening they would never forget.

~ ~ ~

I will instruct thee and teach thee in the way which thou
shalt go.
I will guide thee with mine eye.
~ Psalm 32:8 ~

CHAPTER 15
Time To Come Home

While Esther and Hannah had their noses to the grindstone, studying for exams, Eli and Charles planned their trip to Oxford County. Rather than take a horse and buggy, the two men decided to pay a driver. It was the middle of November, and there was no telling what weather might blow in.

Eli was at the Woerner's early that Wednesday morning. It was a bright sunny morning, but the wind gusts promised to turn it into a typical blustery November day. After stabling his horse in the warmth of the barn, Eli backed his two-seater into the drive-in shed, ready for the trip home. With Eli's help, Charles could finish his chores in record time. They trudged up to the house, and the warm smells of breakfast greeted them as they entered the kitchen.

Anna bustled around the kitchen, placing breakfast on the table while her heart thumped anxiously. She nearly collided with Naomi when carrying a bowl of home fries to the table. Naomi looked bewildered at her mother, curious why she seemed so unusually flustered. After that, breakfast continued without incident while the men ate before their driver arrived.

They set their coffee mugs on the table just as a horn honked in the yard. Naomi and Anna came out to see the men off. "Here's a lunch," Anna handed a bag to her husband, and Naomi placed another bag on the seat, setting a thermos beside it. "There are apricot turnovers and *kaffee* if you get hungry before lunch," Anna explained. Both men nodded in acknowledgment. A hint of a smile relaxed the older man's face, and Eli smiled his thanks to Naomi.

"We should be back by four. I left the driver in the barn, in case ya need ta make a trip inta town," Charles looked at his wife.

"Be safe." Anna bade them goodbye and stepped back as the door slid shut on the van. "They'll have a *gut* day," Anna smiled at her daughter as they headed back to the house. "Eli's a nice young *mann*. He and your *Daed* get along real *gut*."

"*Ja*, they do," Naomi nodded, pleased.

"Did Eli tell you where they're going?"

"To some *milching* operation to see how it's set up before he begins setting up his own," Naomi returned.

"*Ja*, that's true, but it's an operation your *bruder*, Charles manages up in Oxford," Anna let out an apprehensive sigh.

Naomi stared at her mother, and her jaw dropped. "It's been years since we've seen Charles." She collected herself and closed her mouth before being corrected for the unladylike gape.

"Three years, seven months, and twelve days." Tears formed in Anna's eyes. "I know *Gott* has a plan." She whispered her response because the emotion she felt was so great that she had difficulty talking.

"Do you suppose he might *kumme* home?" Naomi dared to ask.

"The farm is getting too much for your *Daed to run alone*." Anna took a handkerchief out of a fold in her choring apron and mopped at her eyes. "Let's pray he does *kumme* back and takes over the farm. That would be an answer to prayer, *Ja*?"

"*Ja*, it would. Then Hezekiah, then Hiram and Leah," Naomi added excitedly. "Maybe they'll *kumme* home too."

"We can only pray. Your *bruders* Charles and Hezekiah always sent me letters, and Leah too, but I have no idea where Hiram is. All I can do is hope and pray that *Gott* will guide and protect him and that he is well. *Kumme*, we need to get inside; all this talk of my lost *kinder* makes me too emotional."

Naomi took hold of her mom's hand. "Some hot tea might go *gut* right now, *Ja*?"

"*Ja*," her mother agreed, and they walked up the steps to the house, deep in their own thoughts.

~.~.~.~

Charles gave their driver the address they were going to. Watching while the man pulled out his maps of southern Ontario and pushed a couple of buttons on the dashboard, Charles shook his head. 'The *Englisch* rely too much on machines.' He turned back to hear what Eli was saying about not understanding how the English did things. "*Ja*." He agreed. "I can't see doin' without horses. I guess automobiles have their place when ya have ta go any distance, but I don't have much faith in them." Charles changed the subject, "Where did ya *kumme* from before ya got adopted?"

"A part of Toronto called Mississauga."

"Do ya ever think about goin' back there?" It was a question Charles had been itching to ask Eli for a long time.

Eli became thoughtful. "Well, all my people got killed in a fire, an' it ain't my way of livin'. I'll never get farmin' outa my blood. *Nee*. This is where I want ta be."

Charles nodded, satisfied. He didn't want Naomi to go away to live in a big city.

The driver steered his van into a massive dairy operation by ten thirty.

"Where on earth do we start?" Eli looked out the van window. He ogled at the barns, the fields of milking cows, the silos, and all the equipment needed to run the enormous farm.

"I'd say with him," Charles nodded toward a man in his early forties striding from the barn toward them. The man was short and stocky, garbed in the usual Amish attire - a straw hat, blue shirt, and wide suspenders attached to trousers.

Charles climbed out of the van and spoke with their driver. "Pick us up around one thirty or two. We should be ready ta go by then." He placed some bills on the passenger seat beside the driver and turned toward the approaching man. "*Wie gehts*?" He nodded, "Charles Woerner, from down Aylmer way."

"I'm *gut*." The other man reached forward to shake his hand and introduced himself.

"We came ta see yer operation. This here is Eli Kuepfer; he just bought a farm an' wants ta look at some *milchin'* operations before settin' his up."

"Ya *kumme* a long way fer that," the other man laughed. "I'll get my foreman; he can show ya around." He looked closely at Charles. "Are ya kin?"

"He's my *sohn*." Charles returned without elaborating further.

"He's the best herdsman I've ever had. Ya raised him right, I'd say."

"*Danke*," Charles stood a little taller.

"I hope yer not here ta take him with ya. I'm not sure I could replace him, although my boy has been learnin' real gut."

Charles said nothing, just nodded his head.

"There he is now. One of the heifers calved in the field last night." Eli followed his gaze and saw a young man carrying a newborn calf across his shoulders. Close behind, a young cow followed him.

"*Kumme*, I'll get the calf, an' he can show ya 'round," the man invited.

They walked toward the field. Charles Woerner's son set the calf on the ground. "It's a nice bull calf," he announced to his boss before looking up.

"Charles, I guess there's no need ta introduce this *mann*," he nodded toward the elder Woerner. "But this is Eli Kuepfer from down Aylmer way. He's settin' up a *milchin'* operation an' wants ta see this one."

Charles Jr. stood up straight, faced his dad, and said one word as he nodded in acknowledgment. "*Dat.*"

"*Wie gehts*?" Charles Sr. asked.

"*Gut*," the younger Woerner returned, his face devoid of expression.

The owner of the farm looked from one to the other and cleared his throat. "Charles, if'n ya have a few minutes, would ya show them the operation?"

"*Ja*," Charles Jr. nodded and led them to the stable. "I'll show ya the *milchin'* platform first." He showed them through the barn, bright and airy, the walls whitewashed. "We keep the calves outa the main barn; that way if'n there's a scour outbreak, it don't contaminate the main barn." Next, he took them to long low housing with three calves per pen.

"I noticed ya keep a bull," Eli commented.

"*Ja*. They have their place but fer the most part, we use AI."

Charles Sr. raised his eyebrows at that piece of information. "Ya don't see Artificial Insemination bein' used on many Amish farms."

"It keeps from too much inbreedin'. That way, we can keep our best heifers," his son explained.

Charles Sr. nodded his head in understanding, while Eli raised his eyebrows, finding that piece of information invaluable. He stored that piece of wisdom away for when his operation was up and running.

"I'll show ya the fields. We rotate the crops yearly and let one field lay fallow each year; it helps the ground rest instead of bleedin' it all the time of nutrients."

Eli and Charles Sr. nodded, impressed.

"I expect ya can stay fer lunch?" Their tour guide asked.

"*Ja, das gut*," Charles Sr. agreed. "Otherwise, yer *Mamm* packed lunch fer us."

"How is *Mamm*?" The younger Woerner asked.

"*Gut*, real *gut*. Ya should *kumme* an' visit."

"*Ja*, I'd like that. Let me stop by the *haus* an' let Helena know there'll be company fer lunch."

They stopped at the Forman's house, a long ranch-style building, and waited while Charles Jr. went inside. Eli and the elder Woerner stood outside and looked at the grazing cattle in the fields.

The screen door opened, then shut with a bang. "*Dat,* this here is my *frau,* Helena."

Both Eli and Charles Sr. turned and nodded toward a thin flaxen-haired girl. Eli guessed she was in her early twenties.

"This is Mary," Charles Jr. put his hand on a toddler's head. "And this is Charles," he wore a pleased smile at a baby less than a year old.

"Ya have a right fine family," Charles Sr. nodded.

Little Charles looked at Eli and Charles Sr. and opened his mouth in a huge grin.

"We'll take him ta the field with us while ya pull lunch tagether," Charles Jr. said to Helena.

"In an hour or so, then?" She looked up at him with soft violet eyes.

"Make it one an' a half. Ya never can tell what we'll get inta."

Helena nodded at him, took Mary's hand, smiled at Charles and Eli, and went back into the house.

Little Charles held his hands out to Charles Sr.

"He's real sociable," Charles Jr. commented. "Ya don't need ta carry him if'n ya don't want, or if'n he gets too heavy, let me know."

"It's been a long time since I held a *boppli,*" Charles Sr. took the baby in his arms. "My word, what are ya feedin' him? He's some heavy," Charles Sr. smiled at the little guy. Little Charles smiled up into the older man's eyes. "I never thought I'd see the day I'd hold one of my *sohn's kinder*."

"*Ja*. I guess time stands still for no one," Eli agreed. "How does it feel ta be a *Dawdi*?"

"*Gut*, right *gut*," Charles Sr. beamed. He looked over at his son. "When yer ready ta take over the farm, it's there waitin' fer ya."

Charles Jr. stood and looked at his dad. "I guess we always figured it'd be that way, ain't so?"

"We did. Ya have been gettin' lotsa *gut* practice runnin' this operation."

"*Ja*. But eventually, my boss's *sohn* will take over runnin' the farm," Charles Jr. informed them.

"He has a *gut* teacher," Charles Sr. looked at his son and nodded.

"I guess 'cause I learned from one," Charles Jr. smiled fleetingly at his dad.

"Just say when yer *kummin'*. In the meantime, I'll have a *Dawdi haus* built fer yer *Mamm* an' me, an' ya can have the main *haus*."

"*Danke, Dat*. Hezekiah is talkin' about settlin' down. I was talkin' ta him a few weeks back," Charles Jr. commented.

"I'm not sure the farm could support three families, *sohn*," Charles Sr. replied with concern.

"Once I get my farm up an' runnin', might be he could help me," Eli intervened.

"*Ja, das gut*. I'll tell him, an' he can help us move an' *kumme* with us."

"*Ja, das gut*," the older man agreed, pleased.

"How about next spring? It'll give ya time ta build the *Dawdi haus*, get through the winter, an' time fer my boss's *sohn* ta get situated."

"*Ja*, an' it'll give me a chance ta get my operation up an' runnin'. That way yer *bruder* will have a job ta *kumme* ta." Eli announced.

"Yer *Mamm* will be right pleased," Charles Sr. assured.

"It'll be *gut* ta see her again," Charles Jr. nodded; a distant look crept into his eyes.

~ ~ ~

Train up a child in the way he should go,
When he is old he will not depart from it.
~ Proverbs 22:6 ~

CHAPTER 16
Home for Christmas

Christmas break for Fanshawe College students was almost three weeks that year. Esther and Hannah went into their holiday break with vastly different outlooks. Esther was happy to spend some time with her family, but Hannah was pensive. She didn't look forward to the enforced break from newfound friends.

Esther immediately renewed family ties, chatting with her mother and grandmother. They talked about their favorite seasonal recipes. In some, they changed the ingredients; in one, they added orange zest while omitting a spice in another. Decisions were made about which cookies they would bake and which recipes would be more suited to the elderly and the shut-ins. Along with cookies, spicy minced meat pies were baked. The wonderful aroma's in the kitchen encouraged the men to take unplanned trips to the house. They were rewarded with molasses cookies one day, or there might be delicious gingerbread cookies to be consumed on another. But always, they came away with a delicacy baked up by the Kuepfer women.

One day, during a break in their baking, Esther walked across the road to the Yoder farm to visit with her Aunt Miriam. She carried a package of cookies and knocked brightly on the door before letting herself in. "*Hallo, Tante*!" She called out. "I've *kumme* visiting."

Miriam was delighted to have a young person in the house again and encouraged Esther to share about her days away at school. Esther asked about Miriam's girls when she became exhausted talking about herself. "Are Ruthie and Rachel *kumming* home for Christmas?"

Miriam's eyes lit up. "*Ja*. For certain, Ruthie but Rachel lives too far away to make the trip. Now they are living up in the Kawartha's; we don't get to see them."

"Does she write?" Esther looked closely at her aunt.

"*Ja*. All the time. Her little one is growing. Tobiah thinks we can fit a visit in this *kumming* summer. It'll take most of the day to get there, but we can stay with them for nothing once we're there." Miriam smiled at the thought of seeing her eldest daughter again.

"How about Rosie, *Tante*? Do you ever hear from her?" Even though she knew Rosie's leaving was a sensitive spot with her aunt, Esther was curious.

Miriam's face turned grey. She stood up and went to the stove with the pretense of getting them more coffee with the cookies Esther had brought. "*Nee*. I haven't heard from Rosie for almost a year now."

"I'll keep praying for her," Esther offered.

"*Danke*. Pray that one day, she'll *kumme* home. More than anything, I want her to *kumme* home. Until she does, it would be ever so nice if she wrote or got in touch with us to say she's okay."

"I will," Esther promised. "I miss her a lot."

"Me too," Miriam heaved a heavy sigh. "Me too." Changing the subject, Miriam brightened. "Did your *Mamm* tell you we are all having Christmas together?"

"*Ja*. She did. I'm really looking forward to seeing Ruthie again."

"It'll be like *alt* times," Miriam agreed. "Only, we won't go to the pond. It'll be too cold for that."

They both laughed at the idea of having Christmas at the pond.

Esther made it back home before dinner preparations started, so she and Eva chatted while they worked on a new quilt. She shared what she had learned in the marketing class at college, hoping that it would help sell their products. "We could start a cottage industry," Esther ran on, excitedly sharing her ideas. "That way, everyone can pool their crafts so that it won't be such a heavy workload on one or two people. And that way," she paused, taking a breath, "all The People will benefit."

Eva listened and nodded, taking in all of Esther's ideas. Enthused with everything Esther had told her, she brought the subject up at the supper table, and Jed got in on the brainstorming. The more they talked about it, the more sense it made to him. "I'm going to get Tobiah in on this one. He'll know where to begin."

No sooner had Jed relayed Esther's idea than Tobiah repeated, "a place where The People can display handcrafted items. Hmm," he paused, thinking hard on a new business prospect. "Someplace, The People will be seen. Someplace where the whole community will benefit. It's a *gut* idea," he squinted thoughtfully at Jed. "An' it makes a lota sense, but where ta begin?"

Right away, Tobiah began jotting down points on a sheet of paper. Later, he and Jed went for a drive, scouting possible buildings within or near Aylmer. An old textile factory sat empty on Aylmer's Main Street; it had employed many townspeople at one time to produce hockey equipment. Now, it was unproductive and beginning to become an eye-sore. When the two men returned from their excursions, Tobiah got on the office phone, contacted the town hall, and booked an appointment.

Later, approaching Aylmer's city council, Tobiah carried with him a proposition. A convincing proposition. "Rather than let the *alt* historic building continue to deteriorate, sell or lease it to the Amish. It's only causing the taxpayer's money," he contended. "And eventually, you'll have to tear it down, anyway. But if you let us have it, we will restore it, keeping a part of Aylmer's heritage alive." The argument, 'In favor of keeping Aylmer's past alive,' won over the city council. Exactly one week before Christmas, Yoder Mills Inc. bought the old factory for a song in record time. Later, Tobiah rubbed his hands together. 'Wait 'til I tell everyone at our Christmas meal. I can only imagine Esther's response. After all, she was the one that got the ball rolling.'

On a Saturday evening just before Christmas, Thomas drove Esther home following the youth singing. She chatted about her schooling and the baking they'd done for Christmas. "Does your *Mamm* bake for the elderly and shut-ins, Thomas?"

He snorted in disbelief. "We never had food enough fer us. Bakin' fer others was outa the question."

"Does your family do anything special at Christmas time?" Esther pried gently; since it seemed to be a sensitive subject with Thomas.

"Naw. *Dat* says only heathens celebrate Christmas."

"*Ach*," Esther looked at him uneasily; this was a side of Thomas she had never seen before. She changed the subject back to her time in college with Hannah.

"Is that all ya do? Talk?" Thomas criticized, annoyed with her endless prattling.

Esther, hurt to the quick, apologized. "I'm sorry, Thomas. I didn't mean to offend you." She clammed up, having a hard time keeping her emotions in check. When he pulled his buggy up to the foot of the Kuepfer drive, she asked, "Would you like to *kumme* in for something hot to drink?"

"Naw. I'll get on my way," he looked at the road ahead.

"Would you like to *kumme* eat with us on Christmas?" She asked meekly, not wanting to upset him further.

"Naw. Ezekiel asked me ta eat with them."

"Mary Lou's *daed*?" Esther asked, confused that he would eat with Mary Lou's family and not with them. After all, he was betrothed with her, not Mary Lou.

"*Ja*. He's learnin' me ta shoe horses. So, it's only right. Besides, yer place is too far ta *kumme* in the cold."

"Will we go driving tomorrow?" Esther asked, trying to be congenial.

"Naw. Like I said, it's too cold. I best get goin'." He looked at her pointedly, with an unreadable and blank look. Esther noticed how his mouth twisted and wondered if it was his attempt at a smile that didn't quite reach his eyes. She climbed down from the buggy and looked up at him, wondering what she had done wrong or said, that he had become so aloof with her.

"*Danke* for the drive home, Thomas."

"*Ja*." He slapped the horse with the lines and left Esther standing at the foot of the drive. It never occurred to him to watch and make sure she got at least part way to the house safely.

Esther, deflated, began walking up the drive. Red warning signs started going off in her head. But ever optimistic, she rationalized. 'It really is awfully cold for driving.' But something niggled in her thoughts. 'That's what blankets are for, ain't? To snuggle under and keep one another warm?'

She remembered earlier that week when she, Eli, and Naomi had carried some baked goods to the elderly and shut-ins. Eli had brought two thick lap robes to protect them from the cold while riding in the buggy. 'So why can't Thomas do the same?' She trudged up the snow-packed lane, repeatedly replaying Thomas's criticism of her trying to fill the conversational void. She recalled when they had delivered the baked goods, that more than anything, just by talking and visiting, they were helping others to overcome their loneliness. 'Is that what life is going to be with Thomas? No one to talk to?' Pushing negative thoughts aside, she entered the warmth of her family home.

The Christmas meal saw the Kuepfer's and Yoder's gathered around the feast-laden table. Tobiah shared his news that he had purchased the old building, and in the new year, it would become the business Esther had inspired. It was the best Christmas gift ever because it had the potential to benefit so many of The People. Esther was beside herself with joy at Tobiah's news; it would be an excellent place for her and her mom to showcase their quilts. Going to college for *rumspringa* was proving to be a worthy investment.

After Christmas, Esther saw Thomas once more at their Sunday Meeting. She approached him to ask if he was going to the singing, but before she could reach his buggy, he dismissively nodded at her and drove away without a second look. Not once during the remaining days she had left of the Christmas and New Year break did he stop by to ask her to go driving with him. In utter bewilderment, Esther went over and over the different times they'd spent together. For all the world, she couldn't imagine what she had said or done that had caused this rift. 'Maybe, once he's working and bringing in money, he'll change,' she thought. Relieved she had figured out what his problem might be, Esther packed and got ready to return to college. She and Hannah were entering their second semester. After that, she'd be back home then she and Thomas could go on with planning their wedding and where they would live. She smiled and packed a token gift for Julia in her bag.

Esther still came home every two weeks and was surprised to see how quickly they progressed at restoring the famous old landmark in Aylmer. The men worked through the cold, first stabilizing the building so that the massive project was complete by the end of February. The People proved their support of the business by quickly

providing items to sell; Amish-made furniture was sold,
along with hundreds of handcrafted items.

Whenever Esther came home, her expanding
knowledge of marketing and advertising was put to good
use in helping grow the new business. It became a voice
for The People without the community becoming involved
with the public.

~ ~ ~

He that hath pity upon the poor lendeth unto the LORD:
And that which he hath given will he pay him again.
~ Proverbs 19:17 ~

CHAPTER 17
New Ideas

Esther and Hannah went back to College the Monday following the new year. Some of their new Night School choices differed after finishing their typing class. While Esther decided nutrition would be an exciting subject to explore, Hannah selected theology.

"Theology? Why theology?" Esther asked, confused.

"Because I want to learn what other religions teach," Hannah shrugged. "When we finish classes in the spring, I don't want to regret I never took the class when I had a chance. Isn't that what *rumspringa* is all about?"

"I suppose," Esther agreed good-naturedly.

In nutrition, Esther and her classmates began by examining human anatomy. Esther found it intriguing that her teeth were more suited for grinding nuts and grains. Their instructor added. "The stomach acids of humans were meant to break down ground food, never to digest animal proteins. As well," she explained, "those on herbivore diets, on average, live seven years longer than do omnivores."

Esther was intrigued. She didn't always believe something just because someone said it was so. The argument that convinced her the most was the evening their instructor told them. "Did you know shrimp can take five to seven days to clear your body? Imagine all the toxins your body is dealing with while trying to digest it. Not to mention the unnecessary energy your body requires to deal with those toxins."

Esther hadn't thought of it in that context before, not that shrimp was ever a part of her diet. But just knowing the fact was interesting to her. When she returned to Julia's that evening, she looked up the diet God had initially intended for man to eat. Turning in the Bible, she read:

And Gott said, I have given you every herb bearing seed...
and every tree which is the fruit of the tree
~ Genesis 1:29 ~

The nutritionist was correct. Then why did people eat meat, and where had it originated. She searched Bible scripture again to find out when man first began eating meat.

Every moving thing shall be meat for you
~ Genesis 9:3 ~

'But that was only after the flood because there were no herbs or nuts to eat,' Esther realized. 'And even Jesus and His disciples ate fish, at least according to the Bible they did.'

In the book of Leviticus, Esther read about the animals God considered clean. Then she read about those He considered unclean. 'Then why do people keep eating meat instead of *Gott's* intended diet?' So, the next day she went back to school with that question.

The nutritionist smiled. "I see you have been doing your own research." The instructor presented the question to the class.

"That's easy," a young woman answered. "Connect the dots on what we have learned in this class. Start with the fact that our bodies were never meant to consume meat. And given that prolonged use of meat is toxic to our system, I'd say there is a reason God allowed us to continue eating it."

That set the wheels turning in Esther's brain. 'Did *Gott* allow the consumption of meat to shorten our lifespans? Methuselah lived nine hundred, sixty-nine years, and man now only lives sixty-five to eighty-five years. That's a big difference! If man reverted to an herbivore diet, would they begin to live longer? It's an interesting theory,' Esther contemplated. One she intended to examine closely. 'One more thing to talk with *Mamm* and *Dat* about when I go home again,' she added to her mental note-taking.

In the next nutrition class, their instructor prepared them for baking. She began by discussing the ingredients they would work with to make a pie. "How many have done any cooking or baking?"

Esther chuckled to herself but looking around the room, she was shocked at how few hands were raised. It had never occurred to her that people outside the Amish community weren't big on cooking. 'Then what do they eat?'

Their teacher also looked around at the class. "The first thing we are going to talk about are measurements. In Canada, we use the Imperial System of measurement. For our use, we will be using cups to measure dry and liquid measurements. You will also use measuring spoons for measurements; tablespoons, teaspoons, and smaller units of the teaspoon. Some bakeries weigh their ingredients; it is a more accurate measurement. But most homes do not have scales small enough to weigh ingredients. So, to simplify our class, we will use the cup and teaspoon for baking."

Everyone examined the measuring units. Again, Esther giggled to herself. 'At home, we bake every day. I never imagined some people wouldn't know what to do with measuring cups or spoons.'

The instructor showed everyone how to measure shortening accurately. "If your recipe calls for a one-half cup, begin by selecting a two-cup measuring unit. Fill the unit to the one-cup level with the water. Then, place shortening until the water reaches the one-and-a-half cup level. Pour off the water, and the shortening will measure exactly one-half of a cup.”

Esther was intrigued and gave it some careful thought. She finally concluded that this method of measurement made sense. After all, the shortening was displacing the water. And since the water had nowhere to go but up, it would be an accurate measurement. 'One more thing to share with *Mamm* and *Mammi*.'

Esther and Hannah often went to the mall in London's south end following their classes. They looked through shop windows at the clothes on sale; most catered to the young women with lacey and gauzy blouses that could be seen right through. Hannah picked up some mint-colored cotton shorts.

"They don't give much room for the imagination, do they?" Esther whispered, shocked.

Hannah examined them. "I kinda like them."

"Where would you ever wear them? Not to school. And definitely not home." Esther asked, bewildered.

Hannah shrugged. "I don't know. I just like them."

Esther, more conservative, looked at a dark green skirt embroidered with green silk.

"Are you going to buy that skirt? Because I want to buy these shorts." Hannah decided.

"I'm not buying. We just came to look. Remember?" Esther began walking down the mall. "Besides, we better get going. Julia will have supper waiting on us."

Hannah's evening class seemed to last longer than Esther's as the days wore on. Esther was mystified about where Hannah went and what kept her out so late. Hannah never said, and Esther could only imagine her answer if she did ask. Something along the line, 'Isn't that what *rumspringa* is all about?' Regardless, they still attended their college classes and ate lunch together. The cafeteria was a great meeting place for students attending college. One day, Esther met one of Hannah's friends.

"Esther, this is Joe." Hannah looked at her new friend, dreamy-eyed. "He takes the same theology class I signed up for."

Esther looked from one to the other, thinking. 'Oh – oh! This can't be *gut*. How am I going to explain her getting involved with an *Englischer*?' Instead, manners superseded any misgivings, and she smiled at Hannah's friend. "Are you going to be eating with us today?"

"I sure am." Joe smiled; his eyes crinkled with merriment. It was a smile of deference, and it lit up his whole face.

Instantly, Esther liked him. They went through the lineup and got lunch. Carrying their trays to an empty table, they talked about their classes. Naturally, the conversation turned toward theology. Esther was enthralled with what Joe had to say about Bible teachings; she added it to her mental log along with the other information her mind was stockpiling.

One Monday in March, a group of students from the Arts Department swept everyone along in their airs of theatrics. Trish, the student council spokesperson and the group's self-appointed leader stood on a chair in the centrally located cafeteria. She put her hands up to stop the laughing and joking, "Everyone listen! I have an announcement. You know how they say everyone has a look-alike?"

Everyone nodded their heads in agreement.

"We have someone right here! Right now, that's Twyla Laine's double!"

"Twyla Laine!" Everyone ogled, unbelieving. Some laughed, thinking it was a joke.

"Not THE famous country and western singer?" Someone shouted out. Excitedly, students began examining one another. Did someone, anyone amongst their friends, look remotely like Twyla Laine?

"Who is Twyla Laine?" Esther frowned at Hannah.

"I haven't a clue," Hannah admitted with a shrug.

"She's a famous country and western singer," Joe informed them.

"Give up?" Trish challenged everyone. The students looked at her as if she had suddenly sprouted two heads. Stepping off the chair, Trish walked purposefully toward Esther and Hannah. "Here she is and pointed toward Esther.

Esther, horrified, wished she could shrivel up and hide. It didn't matter where! Under a table or chair, she would have given anything to be somewhere else at that precise moment.

As if in unison, everyone shook their heads and frowned at Trish.

"Look," Trish pointed out. "Take off the glasses," she demanded of Esther and held her hand out for them.

Under the scrutiny of everyone, Esther removed her glasses but held onto them.

"Look," Trish pointed to a poster behind Esther. "Same nose, same hair. Now, do you believe me? She really does look like Twyla Laine!"

Her attitude was infectious. Everyone consulted the poster advertising Twyla Laine performing at Von Kuster Hall - the music atrium at the University, which hosted many great artists in concert. The students looked from Esther to the poster and then back again. In robotic unison, they nodded their heads while comparing the poster with Esther.

"Let's go to the concert and take Esther. Maybe, we'll get a backstage audience with Twyla Laine," Trish encouraged everyone.

Mob mentality is always infectious. All the students agreed with the exception, of course, Esther. She didn't want to be caught up in this movement. She did everything she could think of to back out of going, but they wouldn't accept her 'no' for an answer. She was their ticket to get backstage to see the infamous Twyla Laine.

"We'll go Friday afternoon," Trish informed everyone while they excitedly talked at once. "I have tickets to sell if anyone can't get any. So, make sure you're here Friday," Trish instructed. "We'll meet here and go together."

The students dispersed; some headed to classes while others sat and finished their lunch. Esther, Hannah, and Joe were left looking at the poster.

Joe looked from Esther to the poster. "You do look an awful lot alike," he nodded.

"Do you suppose she could be your sister?" Hannah asked, noting how young Twyla Laine looked in the picture. At Joe's confused look, Hannah explained Esther had been adopted.

"Anything's possible," Esther blinked, then stared at the poster. "I never knew my birth, *Mamm*; maybe she had another *boppli* after I was born."

"Well, we'll find out one way or the other on Friday," Hannah assured them.

"Yeah. It could be really interesting," Joe concluded. "Maybe you are twins."

"*Ja*. This could be more than just interesting." Esther agreed, still baffled by this mystery person.

"I wonder if your *mamm* and *daed* know anything about her?" Hannah remarked.

"If they do, they never said anything to me," Esther looked mystified.

"We'll find out Friday," Joe concluded.

"Are you *kumming*?" Hannah asked, looking at him, pleased.

"I wouldn't miss it for the world," he grinned at Hannah.

Esther missed their exchange. She had misgivings about meeting this person everyone was convinced was her look-alike. 'Surely *Mamm* and *Dat* would have said something? We aren't that kind of family to keep secrets, especially of this nature. So, who is Twyla Laine? A happenstance look-alike? A *schwester* I've never met?' Regardless, Esther's stomach was beginning to squeeze with anxiety. She didn't like not knowing about things and being kept in the dark. With a sigh of determination, she straightened her shoulders. 'If I don't go, it will always remain a mystery of who I am. Maybe Twyla Laine can enlighten me on who my real *Mamm* was and why she gave me up for adoption. Maybe she died in childbirth. And maybe she honestly won't know. Well, Friday is D Day. The day this all *kummes* to a head and perhaps a change that could affect my life forever.'

~ ~ ~

We know that all things work together
for good to them that love God
~ Romans 8:28 ~

CHAPTER 18
Twyla Laine

Friday afternoon, everyone met at the college's central cafeteria. Tickets had been purchased before leaving, and those without, bought them from Trish. Before leaving, Esther had one more chance to study the poster. She had to admit, this Twyla Laine did look like her a lot. Or maybe it was the other way about – perhaps she looked like Twyla Laine.

"You two look like you could be *schwesters*." Hannah exclaimed excitedly as she gazed at the poster with her friend.

Trish, always in control, came over to stand beside Esther. "Let's go," she took hold of Esther's hand. Because Esther was holding Hannah's hand, all three girls were swept along with the wave of students, and Hannah was almost jerked off her feet as the crowd surged forward.

Joe laughed and did his best to stay up with them. "I'll see you at the theater," he called out. A rowdy group piled onto city buses and headed to the University's Von Kuster Hall.

Arriving, they waited in line to hand their tickets in at the admission counter. The noise and jostling of the theater crowd made it impossible to hear what anyone was saying. Once they entered the atrium, the chaos was deafening.

They sat down and watched the forty-five-minute opening act, a comedian who afterward introduced Twyla Laine. They watched the singer for an hour before Trish suddenly stood up, anticipating the upcoming intermission. Trish nodded at Esther in the dimly lit theater, motioning for her to follow. Esther looked at Trish baffled but followed - not that she had much choice. Trish still had her in tow. In turn, Esther hadn't let go of Hannah's hand either. Hand in hand, they followed Trish as she led them toward the stage door. "If we get separated, I'll see you tomorrow evening at night school," Joe called to Hannah. She turned to wave to him.

A security guard glared at them, but Trish, not intimidated, went closer and said something, causing him to look closer at Esther. He looked up at the stage at the performing singer and eventually consented with a nod. Esther had no idea what Trish said, but it didn't matter; all three girls were being allowed backstage.

Trish smiled at Esther and Hannah as the security guard held the door open, allowing the three girls passage. With a huge grin, Trish smiled triumphantly. 'What did I tell you?' Aloud she instructed Esther. "When you see Twyla come from behind that curtain, take your glasses off."

Esther did as she was asked, not wanting to be the one to dash cold water on Trish's dream.

"Twyla, I have your look alike," Trish boldly confronted the performer as she came offstage.

Twyla looked at them, shocked. "I don't know how you got permission to come back here," she began, perturbed, before Trish interrupted, pushing Esther forward. Twyla looked at Esther, and her mouth dropped open. It was like looking at herself in a mirror. There was no mistaking their resemblance. They could have been identical twins. Instead of the western hat Twyla was wearing, Esther was bare-headed. Where Twyla's hair was loose, Esther's hair was pulled back in a French braid.

"Come with me," Twyla instructed, leading the girls to a back room with many mirrors, lights, and costumes. Once the door closed behind them, Twyla rounded on them. "What do you want?" She demanded. "Money? A gig? To have your picture taken? I could have you arrested, you know."

"Nothing," Trish shook her head. "We wanted you to see your look-a-like. Everyone has a look-a-like, somewhere in the world," she smiled a little apprehensively. Her enthusiasm began evaporating under Twyla's piercing scowl.

Twyla looked at Trish perturbed, then Esther. "What's your name anyway?" She demanded.

"Esther Kuepfer," Esther answered, horrified that Trish was pushing in on another's privacy. The Amish could appreciate what it meant to have their privacy invaded.

"How old are you, Esther?"

"Seventeen, I'll be eighteen at the end of this *kumming* summer."

Twyla went pale. Even though she wore ample make-up, her paler was evident, and she turned away from the girls. "I want Esther to stay here, and you two girls wait outside."

Trish and Hannah did as they were asked. Before leaving, they looked at Esther optimistically, wide grins on their faces.

Twyla looked at Esther, curious about the young woman before her. They talked awkwardly for a few minutes. Twyla asked her questions about the classes she was enrolled in at the college, and Esther readily answered in her quiet and reserved way. With an attitude that clearly said Twyla Laine was used to getting her way, she announced, "I want you to do something for me, Esther."

"I'll try," Esther agreed, nerves like butterflies flitting around her stomach.

"I need to go back on stage in another ten minutes, and I want you to go with me."

Esther began to protest.

"It would mean more than anything to me. I want to introduce you as my – my sister, Penny. Would you do that for me? You have no idea how important it is to me."

"Can I talk to my friends first?" Esther agreed reluctantly.

"Sure," Twyla smiled and opened the door, and Hannah was invited back into the dressing room.

Esther explained in the dialogue that only she and Hannah understood.

"I'd say, go for it," Hannah smiled excitedly. "Why do you think we're on *rumspringa*? To try out all these different things."

Esther gave her friend a pained look, turned to Twyla, and nodded. 'What am I getting myself into?' She agonized.

Twyla smiled, looked at Hannah, and opened the door suggestively. "We'll be out in a few minutes," closing the door as Hannah left the room.

"Put these clothes on," she demanded and handed Esther a costume.

Esther shook her head, "I don't wear pants."

Twyla looked exasperated and rolled her eyes. Going through her wardrobe of costumes, she insisted. "Put this on, and hurry; the audience doesn't like to be kept waiting. Put this hat on," she instructed. Waving a well-manicured hand toward Esther's head. "And let your hair go."

When Esther shook her head, Twyla compromised. "At least take it out of the braid and let me tie it back with this." She pulled Esther's long hair back with a ribbon.

They stood side by side, looking at their reflections in the mirror. Twyla's face had a mature look and looked a little harassed. 'Most likely the results of show business,' Esther assumed. Otherwise, they were like two peas in a pod, as her grandmother would have said. Before Esther could ask her own questions, a knock sounded on the door.

"You're on, Twyla."

"Let's go!" Twyla smiled at Esther. "Just follow my lead, and remember, your name is Penny, and you're my sister. Don't be afraid." She took Esther's hand in hers. They walked out the door, across the stage, and stood in front of a hoard of strange faces.

Fortunately, Esther couldn't see the crowd at that moment because of the spotlights. Mercifully, she was blinded to all the faces looking at her and Twyla. Twyla introduced her, continued holding her hand, and sang. Afterward, some said it was the best performance she'd ever put on, and she'd never have one equal to it again.

Esther was glad Twyla Laine held her hand on stage, or she would have melted from fright before the very crowds Twyla lived to perform.

After the performance, Esther quickly changed out of the western costume and replaced it with the quiet, unassuming clothing, similar to The People's. This life of performing was not where she wanted to be - she preferred the quiet country life of the Amish. The lights held no appeal for her, nor did the noise of strange people whistling and clapping at her.

Twyla smiled and thanked her. "You do know who I am, don't you, Penny?"

"*Ja*, Twyla Laine. My *schwester*?" Esther smiled, although her head was throbbing from the lights, the noise, and the tension. Now it was time to ask some long-awaited questions. Before she could ask even one, Twyla laughed and smiled kindly at Esther.

"You got part of it right. I am Twyla Laine. But you aren't my sister - you're my daughter." Twyla informed gently, hoping the revelation wouldn't be too much of a shock to this girl standing before her.

Esther snatched her hand away as if she'd been burned. "*Nee*," she gasped, and tears gathered in her eyes.

Twyla nodded her head. "Yes. I've been looking for you, everywhere."

"But why did you give me away?" Esther agonized.

"It's a long story. But in a nut-shell, I knew I could never raise you and have a career too."

"So, you chose a career over me? Your own flesh and blood?" Esther demanded, swiping at tears streaming down her face. It occurred to Esther how stark the quiet life of The People was compared to this *Englisher's* way of life. One was family first, the other, self-first.

"Try to understand. It was better this way, better for you," Twyla tried to reason.

Esther gulped and stepped away. "I'm not feeling very *gut*. Please call Hannah."

Twyla looked at her, gave a remorseful sigh, opened the door, and asked Hannah to come in.

"We need to go," Esther grabbed Hannah's hand.

"What's wrong? You look *krank*." Hannah held Esther's hand and looked at Twyla Laine, wondering what the older woman had done to her friend.

"I don't feel very *gut*." Esther allowed Hannah to lead her out of the concert hall quickly and through the throng of alien faces. They got on a bus and eventually ended up at Julia's, the trip remaining a blur for Esther.

The next day, Esther left a message on the answering machine in the phone shanty, asking her dad to come to pick her up. She used the excuse, "I'm finished with classes, and I want to *kumme* home."

When Hannah returned from shopping that afternoon, she brought the Saturday edition of the city's paper with her. Pulling out the center of the Entertainment Section, she showed Esther the front page. "No matter what you do, you need to keep this," Hannah made her promise and packed it in with Esther's textbooks. "I'm not going home with you; I want to stay and finish my semester. I'll see you when I *kumme* home on the weekends." She gave Esther a big hug, a hug Esther was to remember for the rest of her life.

~ ~ ~

The Lord is near to the brokenhearted and saves the
crushed in spirit
~ Psalm 34:18 ~

CHAPTER 19
Home to Stay

At noon Jed arrived in a rental van.

"What has happened, *Tochter*?" He searched her face for an answer as they carried her belongings to the waiting van.

"Can we talk about it later, *Dat*? I don't feel very *gut*."

"Not *krank*, are ya?" He persisted after closing the sliding door to the van, and the seatbelts were snapped together.

"*Nee*, just a terrible headache." Esther closed her eyes, trying to escape the bright sunlight and the horror of a world she had been thrust into. 'I didn't ask to be born, and I don't want anybody bothering me,' she convinced herself but retracted. 'Well, maybe *Dat* and *Mamm*, and Eli too. Of course, not *Mammi* and *Dawdi*, but I don't care if I never see anyone else, ever again.' A huge tear rolled down her cheek. A gentle finger brushed it away. Peeking between swollen eyelids, she saw her dad's concerned look. "I'm okay, *Dat*," she attempted to reassure him, closed her eyes, and laid her head on his shoulder.

When the driver pulled into their drive, Esther saw her mother waiting on the porch. She repeated what she had told her dad. "*Mamm*, I have a terrible headache. Can we talk later?" Eva bustled around, helped her get into a nightie, and tucked her into her bed. The last thing Esther remembered was thinking as she fell asleep. 'I never thought I'd miss my bed so much.' She slept until she smelled the coffee perking on the wood stove the following morning.

Esther got up, dressed, and made her way downstairs. Sooner or later, she knew she needed to tell her parents what had happened. From experience, she knew sooner was always better than later.

Solemnly, Esther helped prepare breakfast. Sitting down for breakfast, she pushed her food around on her plate and took a mouthful of coffee. She was glad when Eli and her grandfather made an excuse to go outside. Jed looked at Eva, and they both looked at Esther. He held his hand out to her. "*Kumme*, we will sit in the other room. There was snow last night, an' it's too cold ta sit on the porch."

"*Ja, Dat*. But first, I need to get something from my room." She trudged heavily up the steps to get the newspaper article Hannah made her promise to keep. She didn't look at it but left it folded and handed it to her dad. He looked at her puzzled, unfolded the English paper, and read the contents. He looked at the picture and, without making any comment, handed it to Esther's mother to read.

"This is your *schwester*?" Eva asked, confused.

"*Nee*," Esther shook her head. She didn't think she could squeeze out another tear even if someone paid her to do it. "I can't imagine why she gave me up for a career."

Eva went pale and looked imploringly at Jed.

Jed met Eva's devastated expression, instantly knowing who the woman in the paper was. "Right now, it may not be much of a consolation ta ya, but if'n she hadn't, ya wouldn't be here with us taday. As far as that goes, ya might not have made it at all. She may have been yer birth *Mamm*, but you are our *tochter*. That's somethin' nobody can take from ya or us," Jed patted her consolingly on the back.

"I know *Dat*, but that still doesn't stop it from hurting."

"*Ja*, an' I expect it will fer some time. But remember, we are family, an' family is always there fer each other. And it doesn't change the love we all share." He stood up and placed the newspaper article under the family bible. "I guess I need ta get out ta the barn." He looked over at Eva and nodded. She returned the nod and stood up to return to the kitchen.

"*Mammi* and I are making pies. Do you want to help us, Esther?"

"*Ja, Mamma*." Esther followed her out to the kitchen.

As one day turned into another, she went through the motions of everyday living. Esther hardly ate, and she never went out. She became a recluse. When anyone came to the house, she disappeared upstairs or went outside. Eventually, her brother cornered her while she was hanging clothes on the line.

"Thomas has been askin' after ya," Eli leaned back on the rail fence while watching her.

Esther continued hanging their dad's shirts. "I don't want to see him," she returned shortly and kept her back to Eli.

"*Ja*. Ya need ta. He promised ta wait fer ya, an' now ya need ta give him an answer, one way or the other," Eli pushed. He wasn't trying to be bossy, but he knew that if Esther continued to avoid the issue, nothing would get resolved between her and Thomas.

Esther switched to another line and abruptly shoved a peg down on a pair of men's work trousers. Glancing over at Eli, she pulled a face.

"It's the right thing ta do," he insisted.

"*Ja*, I suppose," she muttered. "The next time he comes 'round, I'll talk to him." She escaped up the steps to the back porch leading into the kitchen.

'The next time,' happened two days later, on a Saturday afternoon. "I was wonderin' if'n ya want ta go drivin'?" Thomas looked down at the floor and asked in his usual monotone, unassuming way.

Esther looked over her shoulder at her mother as if for help.

"I'll get your cape and bonnet; it might get cold," Eva bustled about, helping her get ready.

"Can I take the Bible?" Esther asked, deflated, now that all chances for escape were gone, and received a nod from her mother.

If Thomas wondered why she had a Bible, he didn't ask. In fact, he didn't ask her anything, such as: are you comfortable, are you warm enough, or even, how are you today?

They drove for a short while, and not one word was exchanged during that time. Thomas repeatedly flicked the lines on the horse's backside to keep it moving forward. If he noticed her at all, he didn't indicate. The fact that she was unusually quiet didn't seem to faze him either. Finally, he pulled over on a back road alongside a frozen river. Esther couldn't help but think, 'Is this his idea of stopping at a romantic spot?'

Thomas leaned forward, elbows on knees, and looked down at his hands. Clearing his throat, he asked, "I was wonderin' if'n ya gave it any more thought about what we talked about?"

Esther, hesitant, nodded. "About us getting married? *Ja,* I've thought about it, but first, there are two things I need to share with you before I can give you my answer."

Thomas turned his head and looked at her with a frown. "*Ja*?" He looked at her with something close to impatience, or was it irritation?

Esther was shaking as much from the cold as from nerves. Pulling the newspaper article from the family Bible, she muttered. "First, I want you to read this." She handed him the paper.

He read it and shook his head. "I'm not sure what yer gettin' at," with a flick of his wrist, he practically threw the paper back to her.

Esther sighed, 'he isn't making it easy.' "This was me when I was on *rumspringa*."

"*Ja*, says you an' yer *schwester*," he shrugged noncommittally.

"That's what she wants people to think," Esther said bitterly. "Actually, she's my birth *mamm*."

That got his attention. Thomas looked at her with distaste, his lip curling in a sneer. "Ya mean yer *Englisch*?"

"*Ja*, my birth *mamm* was an *Englischer*, but I was raised Amish. I'm adopted."

Thomas sat up straighter – ramrod straight. "Ya was tryin' ta trick me inta marryin' ya - an *Englisher*," he accused and confronted her with it. "Now that's not right, that just ain't right. Ya led me ta believe ya was Amish, and ya ain't!" He gathered up the lines and yanked the horse around, driving Esther home much faster than they had come out.

Esther climbed out of the buggy. "Do you want to *kumme* in and warm up, Thomas?"

"Naw, I'm figurin' that wouldn't be right either – socializin' with an *Englisher* in an Amish *haus*. It don't make no sense ta me. As a matter a fact, that's the same as blasphemy, ta me."

Esther bearly had time to lift the Bible from the seat, and not a moment to soon. Thomas slapped the reins on the horse's backside and was gone. She stood in the cold, watching the buggy disappear down the drive. A huge sigh escaped her; whether from relief or despair, she had no time to analyze because her mom called from the porch.

"Esther, *kumme* in. It's too cold to stand outside."

Esther turned and walked toward the welcoming voice of her mother. '*Dat* is right; family is always there for family.' Tears began flowing down her face. Were they tears of relief? Perhaps. Tears of thanksgiving? Probably. But tears for just having Thomas break their engagement? Never!

Her mother handed her a handkerchief. "I have hot chocolate and oatmeal cookies. At least, I think your *daed* and *bruder* left some on the table."

"*Ja*, that'd be nice," Esther nodded.

"Then we can sit, and you can tell me how your drive went with Thomas," Eva added motherly.

"We don't have to sit for me to tell you – not very *gut*. Depending on how you want to look at it, I guess," Esther answered forlornly.

"What happened?" Eva led her into the kitchen and helped her out of her cape and bonnet.

"When I showed him that newspaper article, he said I was an *Englischer*. And then he said I had been trying to trick him into getting married."

Eva inhaled sharply, shocked, and put her hand to her chest. "He said that to you?" Eva went from shock to anger but was quickly pacified when she realized that Thomas would never hurt her daughter again.

Esther nodded her head. "I didn't even get to ask him how he felt about certain Bible truths, and I asked him to *kumme* in and get warm when we got back. But he said it wouldn't be right socializing with an *Englischer* in an Amish *haus*. Do you suppose that means we're not getting married now, *Mamma*?"

"I expect it does," Eva confirmed Esther's apprehension. Silently, she sent thanksgiving heavenward. '*Danke*, heavenly *Vater,* for looking after my little girl.' She asked, concerned, "How do you feel about this?"

"I'm not sure, *Mamma*. I used to be glad I wasn't going to end up an *alt maidel*. Then, when I look at you and *Dat*, I want to have what you have together, and I knew I never would with Thomas."

"*Ja*, marriage can be very *gut* when you have the right person. Do you know your *Daed* and I have been married for almost thirty years? The best thing you can ask yourself is, would you have been happy living with Thomas that long?"

Esther frowned in contemplation and shook her head sadly, "I don't think so, *Mamma.*"

"Then think about this. It was *gut* you met your birth *mamm*. Otherwise, you wouldn't have had the newspaper picture. Neither would you have learned how Thomas felt about the *Englisch* until it was too late, maybe way too late. Perhaps after having *kinder* and think how he might have treated them."

Esther was stunned as a vision of terrified, neglected children passed before her eyes.

"If someone thought the whole world of you, do you think being Amish or *Englisch* would have mattered? This was *Gott* intervening for you. Don't you think it was rather coincidental you met your birth *mamm*, then had this talk with Thomas? *Nee*, this was *Gott's* doing." Eva nodded, convinced. "There's something else you might consider," she added gently.

Esther's eyebrows went up, confused.

"Someday, you might consider writing your birth *mamm*. Thank her for meeting with you and giving you a chance to grow up in a family. She was very young, probably younger than you are now, and I think she was very brave doing what she did. Deep down, I expect she knew she couldn't provide for you. And seeing you at the concert was probably an answer to prayer. A prayer that she might see you one more time."

Tears rolled down Esther's cheeks. "*Ja*, sometimes someone else can see how it really is, not how it might have been. *Danke, Mamma*."

"Say *Danke* to *Gott*," Eva murmured and rubbed Esther's back lovingly.

"*Ja*," Esther nodded deep in thought and swirled the last of her hot chocolate in the bottom of the mug.

Weeping may tarry for the night, but joy comes in the
morning
~ Psalm 30:5 ~

As spring approached, Esther gave more thought to what her mother had suggested. She felt safe surrounded by her family, away from the mayhem of what some people classify as the norm. Feeling secure, she summoned the courage to write her birth mother. Esther thanked her for being brave in placing her up for adoption. "Deep down, I know you have been praying for me," she wrote. "I know this is *Gott's* way of letting you know I'm well."

She signed it, "Esther." She placed the name her birth mother had given her in brackets, "Penny." Esther researched and found the address to Twyla Laine's next concert, then placed the letter in the mailbox at the end of the drive, with no return address.

Many weeks later, Twyla Laine cut a gold record entitled, "God Answered My Prayer."

Although Twyla looked for an Amish girl by the name of Esther Coffer, she never saw her again. The young girl that had given birth to a baby named "Penny" lived the rest of her life at peace. God had answered her one fervent prayer, that she might see her little girl one more time.

~ ~ ~

For everyone who asks receives,
and he who seeks finds,
and to him who knocks it will be opened
~ Matthew 7:8 ~

And all things you ask in prayer, believing, you will
receive
~ Matthew 21:22 ~

<u>Epilogue</u>

Esther had been confronted with two consecutive life-changing events, and still, she was able to slide back into her old, familiar routine on the farm. Despite withdrawing emotionally, the strength of the Kuepfer family surrounded her and allowed her wounds to heal. Her days became filled with laughter, and she found joy in her return to Amish life. Wash days occupied every Monday, while canning, quilting, and all the chores needing to be done on the farm helped fill the other days. As the months went by and spring became summer, her complexion returned to its former healthy glow.

That summer, the whole Kuepfer household helped Eli move his small herd of Holstein cattle to his new farm. In Eli's absence, Esther pitched in and helped her dad more on the farm, while her grandfather did a little less. Eli and Naomi married the fall that Esther turned eighteen. Among those married during that fall wedding season were Thomas and Mary Lou.

Thomas had been working as an apprentice under Mary Lou's dad. Mary Lou's dad, the smithy for the area, had an invested interest in teaching him the skill of blacksmithing.

He was not one to suffer fools and fully intended Thomas to support his daughter and his future grandchildren.

Life on the Amish farms continued to thrive - family working with family, a world unto themselves. Charles Jr., Helena, and their two small children, moved home to the large Woerner farmhouse. The elder Woerner's moved into the newly built *Dawdi haus*. Hezekiah Woerner finally left his running around years behind him and came home. He worked on Eli's farm, bent on saving enough money to start his own operation raising veal calves. Charles Sr. mellowed when three of his children moved to live near him. He thrived, surrounded by his grandchildren with two more on the way. Naomi's firstborn, Perry, held a special place in her father's heart. The older man was content; life couldn't get much better than that.

Esther never saw Hannah again. Hannah had met and married an outsider. The young man from the theology seminar, Joe. It brought about an overwhelming feeling of guilt for Esther. She often wondered if Hannah would have come home if she had stayed on at the college. Her mother consoled her, "we can't always feel responsible for everyone else. We must all lead our own lives." Eva whispered to her on the side, "Hannah never did her kneeling baptismal vows before *rumspringa*. She may *kumme* home yet." That gave Esther hope that she'd see her friend again one day. To that fact, she prayed for her school friend every day.

~.~.~.~

The spring before Esther turned twenty-two, her parents planned a trip to Florida. Her mother wanted to visit her sister, Eadie. It was the beginning of March, and everyone was convinced it would be an early spring.

"Just think," Eva exclaimed. "By the time we get home, the tulips and crocus will be blooming, and the maple trees will be filling up the pails with sap."

"There's no need to worry about the animals," Jed assured Esther. "Tobiah has promised ta *kumme* over every day and help with the chores. Ya can handle the feedin' mornin' an' in the afternoon, *Ja*?" Jed asked Esther.

"*Ja, Dat*, I know what to do," Esther assured him. She and her grandparents waved her parents off as the van went down the lane. They were headed for Pierson International Airport in Toronto, where they would get a direct flight to Tampa International Airport in Florida.

Esther breathed in the clear spring air while walking beside her grandmother. She was at peace with her life, living as a spinster. Her grandfather hobbled ahead of them as they turned back toward the house. He was intent on getting inside, away from the dampness of the early spring air. Back to his comfortable chair and the heat he applied regularly to his back. They would be fine. They had one another, and family always looked after family.

~ ~ ~

Be strong and courageous.
Do not fear... for it is the LORD your God who goes with you.
He will not leave you or forsake you
~ Deuteronomy 31:6 ~

Are you interested in adopting?

Did you know:

From 1999-2017 there were approximately 271,833 adoptions worldwide.

More than 30,000 orphans have a birthday every year without a family.

Since 2005 the rate of adoptions has slowly decreased.

As of 2017, only 24% of orphans in the foster care system were adopted.

Please contact your local Social Services for more information on adoption. Many churches also provide information on adoption.

Stay tuned for the next story in
The Woodcarver's Quilt series.

A Christmas Rose

By: J. Linde

www.ingramcontent.com/pod-product-compliance
Lightning Source LLC
Chambersburg PA
CBHW061515120726
48001CB00004B/1330